SMALL ACTS
OF COURAGE

SMALL ACTS OF COURAGE

Sue McCormick

TOWN
HEAD
PRESS

For Mark

First published in Great Britain by Townhead Press, 2020
This paperback edition published 2020
Copyright © Sue McCormick

3 5 7 9 10 8 6 4 2

The right of Sue McCormick to be identified as the author
of this work has been asserted in accordance with sections
77 and 78 of the Copyright, Designs and Patents Act, 1988.

Designed and produced by Kate & Ian Craig
Cover photograph © Kate Craig

A CIP catalogue record for this book
is available from the British Library

ISBN: 978 1 5272 6421 2

Printed and bound in Great Britain by 4edge Limited

FOREWORD

WHAT times these are. As I write, we are in the midst of lockdown during a global coronavirus pandemic, and I wonder what history will make of this period of our lives, in particular the stark facts that the crisis has brought into sharp focus: that the way we live and consume has become unsustainable, that our government (and a few notable others) are self-serving, murderous incompetents and that ordinary people will always pay the price for our leaders' mistakes. The term "lions led by donkeys" has been resurrected from the days of World War 1 to describe the incredible key workers and NHS staff who have died needlessly because of our leaders' self-interest and lack of care, that has led to a deadly lack of protective equipment. And again there have been endless attempts to silence those who seek to "politicise" this most political of issues, by the many tried and tested methods that have been rolled out over history: mockery, intimidation, a bombardment of empty patriotism.

Over and over, history offers up its lessons, and over and over, those in power choose the narrative they wish to pass down. So, this wonderful book, written by my friend and comrade Sue McCormick, came at just the right moment for me. Beleaguered by Labour's devastating defeat in 2019's General Election, and finding it painful to constantly imagine how many lives could have been saved if we were living under a government that put its people front and centre of its policies, rather than big business, it has been sometimes difficult in this enforced period of isolation and reflection not to feel hopeless. So, a gallop through our radical history, through the lens of women's unique experience of that history (I've always been fond of the term "herstory" and its attempt to redress the centuries-old bias) was just the ticket. Love stories, comic incidents, tales of tragic loss and courage, all against the backdrop of our struggle: from the fight for votes for women (ALL women), to the General Strike, from the post-war Labour victory and the creation of the NHS to the crushing disappointment of the Blair years, from the Chartists to the Spanish Civil War. This beautifully structured novel interweaves our heroines' stories as we move backward and forward in time: women's solidarity and friendship at the core of every strand. And always with the clear message that we must never allow the disappointments of our own failed struggles to turn to despair, that we must have the courage to remain hopeful, that nothing is ever for nothing. In the words of *Small Acts of Courage*'s Charlie, we must open our hearts to hope again, we must "make peace with the past and fight for the future".

This wonderful book could help you make the first tentative steps towards doing just that.

Julie Hesmondhalgh
May 2020

2003

I often hear voices, though I am no Joan of Arc—if God is there, he keeps his silence. God doesn't speak to me, but others do. They live in my head, judge my actions, measure my achievements and I see the world in shadow as their giant shapes block out the sun.

THE room is hot, even with the balcony doors flung wide open. Margaret slips bare feet out of sandals onto the cool tiled floor. Voices drift up from the pavement café below, old men passing the long afternoon as their fathers did before them, drinking ouzo and water, clicking worry beads. Out at sea, a sailboat is caught suddenly in a dazzle of silver from the low sun.

She had hoped that pen and paper would make it easier, the mineral smell of ink and the motion of her hand more intimate than words on a screen, but the distance she feels is more than land and sea, and emptier. She writes two words—hello love—and he is conjured behind her eyes, a presence almost as familiar as herself, the scent of him, the feel of him, a safe haven. Her yearning rises like a tide, carrying with it the certainty that nothing she can write will be enough.

There is a framed photograph on the wall behind the table, a grainy sepia print of tourists on the beach, a woman in dated swimwear, a man in high-waisted trousers with white shirt sleeves rolled to the elbow. Beyond them, a small girl with a ribbon bow in her bobbed hair is running towards the sea, arms outstretched in excitement. With a sudden, sweet connection to childhood, Margaret remembers the same pose, the same joy and expectation. For a moment, she can feel the wet sand between her toes and the wind on her face. She remembers how it felt to run full pelt towards life. Reflected in the glass, her forty-year-old face stares back at her reproachfully.

The pen is still in her hand, hovering uselessly over the

paper. No words for David but, for herself, a whirl of thoughts and memories, an unfiltered deluge, clamouring for attention.

My sins are beating at the door.

The evening has darkened around her. Outside, the sky above the sea is pink and purple. Pushing the letter aside, she goes down to walk by the water, to watch the last sliver of sun dip below the horizon.

At a taverna by the harbour the waiter brings a jug of water and a basket of fragrant bread, yellow as sponge cake. When the white cloth flaps in the night breeze from the sea, he secures it under a length of string tied tightly round the table-top in readiness. She eats red mullet and a salad rich with olives and salty cheese. A thin cat appears from nowhere as her food arrives, crouching by the table, silent and hopeful. Against advice she feeds it scraps of fish and it eats hungrily with a wary eye guarding its territory.

'You have a soft heart.' The voice from the next table is English and cultured. The old woman looking up from her book is small and smiling.

'I like cats.'

'You like their independence?'

'Yes.'

'That's the usual reason, isn't it? I must say it has no appeal for me.'

'No?'

'Not a bit. I like to need and be needed.' She has a deeply lined face under cropped white hair. Her beaded black dress is swamped by two mismatched cardigans. She lays her book aside. 'Will you join me? Please say yes—I much prefer to eat in company.'

The invitation is unexpected. Margaret wants to say no; small talk is such an effort.

But resistance is even harder.

She caves in and moves across to the offered chair. The cat follows her plate and waits by her feet.

'I'm Margaret,' she says. 'Sorry I can't introduce the cat, I don't know its name.'

'Well I'm less mysterious than that. I'm Charlie. Will you have a glass of wine?'

'No, thank you.'

'Dolmades then? They're delicious.'

She accepts one from the offered plate.

'I confess I hoped we might meet,' says Charlie. 'I've seen you a few times around the island. Is it your first time here?'

'My first time anywhere in Greece.'

'How exciting! You have so much to discover.'

She laughs and tips her glass in acknowledgement before she drinks. There is something of another age about her, another world. Yet, at the same time, she is vividly present. Margaret feels the pull, in spite of herself.

'What are you reading?' she asks.

'Shelley.' Charlie picks up the small, red leather book and shows her the faded gold lettering on the cover. 'There's no-one like him.'

'Look on my works, ye mighty, and despair.'

'You're an admirer too?'

'No-one like Shelley.' They share a smile. Margaret feels the warm evening breeze on her face. She sits back in her chair. The stars are bright in the dark sky over the bay. 'I take it this isn't your first visit?'

'No, my dear. My first stay became an extended one. I live here.' Charlie raises an age-spotted hand and points down the shore. 'That's my house, with the lights on the terrace.'

'What a view!'

'I never tire of it.'

'I envy you. I've always wanted to see Greece. I don't know why it took me till now to get here.'

'Better late than never.'

'Yes.'

'Are you staying long?'

'I don't know—maybe—I'm not sure—'

'Uncertainty? Now it's my turn to envy you.' Charlie's eyes twinkle with self-mockery. 'Life holds few surprises when you get to my age.'

'That isn't always a bad thing.'

'Isn't it?'

Peace and certainty. No more agonising. I would trade anticipation for a quiet mind in a heartbeat. Just to be calm. To be still.

When their plates are empty, the cat leaves, transferring its allegiance to the chargrilled sardines on a nearby table.

'There,' says Charlie. 'That's cat loyalty for you.'

'I had no illusions,' Margaret smiles. She is enjoying the conversation, the level they have set for themselves, a certain formality, a shared understanding.

Charlie pours herself the last of the wine.

'You must go to the mainland if you have the chance. Mycenae, Epidaurus, Corinth, Delphi—'

'I was thinking of taking a trip in a few days.'

'My choice would be Delphi. You can't come to Greece and not see it.'

'The oracle?'

'Where the great questions were asked for centuries.'

Answers from the gods. How simple would that be?

'Delphi it is then.'

'Good. And in the meantime, have you any plans for tomorrow?'

'No, not really.'

'Let me give you lunch then,' Charlie asks. 'Will you?'

Back in her room, the failed letter on the table silently accuses her. She crumples it and throws it into the bin. A moment later she retrieves it, smooths out the creases and puts it back in its place.

That night, she dreams of her twelve-year-old self, a smiling girl in her favourite red dress, her mass of unruly hair tamed in a thick plait. Her wacky hair, David calls it. As a child she had once needed rescuing from high in a tree when loose tendrils caught in the branches, wrapped tight, holding her fast, like Gulliver in Lilliput. Even now, kept sensibly short, it retains its wildness, refuses to conform.

In the dream, she is playing the piano. She is in the dining room of the house she grew up in and dream logic never questions that a piano is there, where one had never been in life. As a child, she didn't know that some houses had pianos and bookshelves with encyclopaedias and poetry, she didn't know that some children were given more than others. Nonetheless, the dream girl sits in her red dress and plays so beautifully that the music stays in Margaret's head when she wakes up in her hotel bed in the half light of a new day.

When I was twelve years old, there was a girl at my school called Roxy. What mystery to be called Roxy! When I heard she was having a baby it seemed fitting. There were echoes of wickedness in her name. Roxy was tasting life. She was vivid, and I was grey. Drab on the outside, hiding blazing, glorious colours within. My shouting, silent self. As a child I claimed the sensation for myself alone. Later, of course, I saw it was a common condition.

When I was twelve years old, I gathered fiction around me like armour, against limitations imposed subtly, in a thousand ways, from birth. To be female, to be working class, to be unexceptional. At my school, the boys took woodwork and metalwork, the girls domestic science and needlework. It never occurred to me to question. I gave it no thought. But now I think of sparks and sawdust and wish it had been different.

*

Charlie's house is simple and beautiful. Antique rugs on the floors, bright art on white walls, shelves of well-worn books. The terrace leads onto the shingle beach and the wide Aegean. Charlie is barefooted and brown legged in an old pair of khaki shorts and the same cardigans as before. There is a mouth-watering display of food on the dining room table.

'Help yourself, my dear. Don't stint.'

'It all looks delicious.'

'I can't take the credit. I get it delivered from around the corner.'

They eat outside. Margaret feels the skin on her shoulders burning. Charlie seems impervious, still wrapped in her cardigans.

'Aren't you roasting?' Margaret laughs.

'In September? This is cool. You should be here in July.'

'Ah, well I'm from the north of England. We're strangers to the sun.'

Charlie has cleared her plate with relish and is leaning back in her chair, cradling her glass of wine. The sea, behind her, is the same colour as the sky.

Azure. Lapis Lazuli.

'Whereabouts in the North?' Charlie asks.

'The Lune Valley.'

11

'It sounds lovely.'

'People think Lancashire is all mills and cobbles and brick terraces. There's plenty of that, to be fair, but some beautiful spots too.'

'My experience was the mills and terraced houses, I'm afraid. But it was many years ago. I spent a few weeks in the little towns around Manchester.' Her eyes light up with amusement. 'In a theatre troupe, no less.'

'You're an actress?'

'Just that once. It was politics. We took a propaganda play to market places and village halls, anywhere we could get an audience. I was with the League of Labour Youth.'

Margaret sits forward.

'Yes, there really was such a thing!' Charlie laughs.

'I know there was. I wrote a feature about it a few years ago, for *The Morning Star*.'

'You're a journalist?'

'Yes—well, I was—I'm not—not now.' A silence threatens. She feels her chest tighten, the blood drumming in her ears. Battling the impulse to take flight, she picks up her plate. 'I'm going to try the moussaka. Can I fetch some for you?'

'I'll do it. You sit tight.'

Charlie pads into the house as Margaret watches the waves, measures her breathing by their rise and fall.

I went in without faith. Why am I so broken by the inevitable?

By the time Charlie comes back with two loaded plates, she is calm again. They carry on as if the moment never happened.

'You're the perfect hostess,' she says.

'Ah, well I was brought up to it, my dear. None of the cooking and cleaning, you understand, none of the work. Just how to look decorative and be amusing—and never speak before the servants. That was the world I was born into.'

'You were lucky.'

'Extremely. My life has been cushioned in ways that most people can never know. I'm what the right-wingers love to call a Champagne Socialist! Do you disapprove?'

'Not if you believe in champagne for all.'

'Oh, I do.'

'So how on earth did you get from that life to the League of Labour Youth?'

Charlie drains the last drops of her wine.

'Ah, that's a long story for another day.'

'No. You can't stop there.'

When Charlie looks up, there is laughter in her face.

'There's method in it, my dear. See how I tempt you to come back?'

*

Harry comes to Charlie in her sleep. He sits on the edge of her bed. She wants to touch his face but is afraid that her hand will pass right through him. That would be unbearable. He looks out of the window.

'Beautiful moon,' he says.

Charlie feels like she's floating away. She tries to think of something solid, something real to anchor her. She remembers Margaret.

'I met a new friend. A comrade. She needs help.'

'Well she's come to the right place.'

'She's lost her way. I can see it in her eyes.'

'Still making things better?'

'What else is there?'

He turns to her and she can see the moon reflected in his glasses, a misty white circle, obscuring his eyes. The ache in her chest swells and deepens.

'I love you, Charlotte West.'

She knows what he wants to hear but she doesn't say it. Of course she loves him. More than life. But if she says it, he might think she has forgiven him.

*

The old bus makes noisy progress up the mountain and, as the driver negotiates the perilous bends with practised ease, Margaret gazes out at the vast sweep of country below. It falls away for miles—parched grassland, olive and lemon groves, clusters of flat-roofed houses and, away in the distance, a glistening sliver of sea. On the other side of the road the ground rises steeply. Craning her neck, she can just about see the gleaming white ruins of Delphi, between the trees.

13

The only other passenger is a woman on the seat opposite. She is cracking pistachios, her feet in a rubble of discarded nutshells. Beside her, a carrier bag bulges with fruit and vegetables, smelling sharp and sweet and of the dry earth still clinging to their roots. Smiling, she leans across the aisle, holding out the bag of nuts.

'Thank you. Efcharistó.' Margaret accepts a handful.

The woman's smile widens. She seems pleased by the attempt at Greek. When the bus stops by a huddle of small houses at the roadside, she gathers her bags and gets off. Eating the green pistachios, Margaret watches her walk to her door, raising a hand as the bus pulls away.

All around, above the pine-clad mountains, the sky is completely, deeply blue.

This same eastern sky spans other lands, not far distant, where guns and shells shatter the quiet, turn cities to dust, break bodies and hearts.

Guilt settles on her again, like a sickness.

Minutes later, the driver rounds the final bend and stops by a small café at the entrance to the site. There is a souvlaki stall, a few chairs and tables scattered in the sunshine and a pair of scrawny brown hens scratching in the dust by the café door. She drinks iced coffee, cold and sweet, and stares with awe at the view. No wonder the ancients gave it such status, worshipped and feasted here, brought sumptuous offerings to the oracle. It feels high enough to touch the feet of the gods and there is something so tranquil, so timeless, that it survives the tourists and the cameras, even the clucking hens at her feet.

In the garden of a house across the road, an old man is cleaning vegetables. He catches her eye and gestures to a wooden chair sitting next to his, at the edge of his plot. Surprising herself, she accepts his invitation.

'English?' he asks as she sits down.

Margaret nods.

'I speak a little.' He smiles a wide, toothless smile. His face is a mesh of brown wrinkles between grey hair and beard. 'I learn from visitors to the ruins. Like you. They sit. We talk.'

'The chair is always here?'

'Every day.' He adds the greens he is holding to the basket at his feet and wipes his palms on his trousers before shaking her hand. 'I am Dimitri.'

'Margaret.'

'You like Greece?'

'Yes. Very much.'

'You like temples? Many temples in Greece.'

'Yes, many.'

'Best here in Delphi.'

She returns his smile. 'Of course. Have you always lived here?'

'Yes. Always here.'

'You've never travelled? Other countries?'

He laughs and spreads his arms to the view and she understands.

When she leaves him, after smiles and handshakes, he goes back to his garden, but he stays on her mind as she wanders through the ancient wonders opposite his house.

A plot of land, a few vines, conversation and a breathtaking view.

He has made his peace, she thinks, and she envies him.

She spends a long time at the Sanctuary of Athena, its three surviving columns shimmering in the heavy heat of late morning, bleached by thousands of years of this same burning sun. It is peaceful. The season is nearly over and she is the only visitor. There is a softness in the silence. Sandaled feet on hot stone, she walks into the sheltering crescent of the columns. In their shadow, she feels suspended in time, feels the continuity of being, for a moment feels a small part of the whole.

Later, as she walks back to the bus stop, she looks across to Dimitri's garden. He isn't there but the door to the house is open and there is a radio playing inside, a folk dance busy with strings and drums. The smell of cooking is in the air, chargrilled meat, garlic and herbs. She imagines him swaying at the stove as the music drifts across the valley. The chair is still sitting at the side of the road.

The bus arrives in a cloud of dust and she climbs on board for the journey back down the mountain. The driver behind the wheel smokes a cigarette. With the hot leather seat sticking to her back and legs, she peers through the dusty window at the columns of the Sanctuary until the last one disappears from sight behind the trees.

*

I'm staying in a room over a bar. At night, I hear music drifting upstairs, a slow bouzouki, rhythmic and joyful. Every night the tables are pushed aside and the locals dance in the small space beside the musicians. Lying alone in the dark, I picture them — arms outstretched, knees bent, fingers clicking — dancing without inhibition, for themselves, for the music.

I miss you, David. Sleeping alone seems strange, wrong somehow. For years we have slept curled together, years of nights with your hand over my heart. I remember as a child, thinking of parents and the sharing of a bed, how inconvenient it would be – an imposition. I remember stretching out my arms and legs, laying claim to space, splayed across my dominions. We yield a lot of territory to love, don't we? Tonight, I feel whole wastelands on either side of me.

*

The terrace is in candlelight, as the moon rises over the sea. There is a concert on the World Service, the aching melody of Elgar's Cello Concerto. Diverted by the music, Margaret isn't prepared for the news headlines that follow. A suicide bomb in Najaf has killed 125 civilians. Sunni and Shia are murdering each other. Iraq is in brutal chaos.

'Can I turn it off?' Her voice is tight.

She reaches across to the radio before Charlie has a chance to answer. Her arm catches the wine bottle and it crashes to the ground. Red wine spatters the tiled floor. She jumps to her feet.

'I'll clean it up. I'm sorry.'

'It's alright.' Charlie's hand is on her arm.

'No. The mess—'

'Be careful. Come away from the broken glass.'

The wine is running in rivulets across the blue and green mosaic. Her feet and legs are splashed with red. She realises she is crying.

'I'm sorry.'

'Don't be.' Charlie moves two chairs to a safe distance. 'Sit down. Tell me what's wrong.' She produces a handful of tissues from a pocket in one of her cardigans. 'Here. Blow your nose, wipe your eyes and tell me.'

It isn't from any hope of relief that she answers.

Absolution shouldn't be that simple.

16

'The war news—'

'Yes?'

'It shouldn't be happening. We shouldn't be there. Our troops, our bombs—'

She is finding it hard to breathe, sucking in air. Charlie moves her chair closer, brushes the hair from Margaret's eyes, strokes her face with the back of a gnarled, brown hand.

'Steady now,' she says softly. 'All is well.'

But it isn't. It never can be again.

She sobs like a child for long minutes, till the panic subsides and her breathing steadies itself. Afterwards, she feels numb, Charlie's eyes are kind and the words aren't impossible to say any more.

'I worked in the Press Office at Downing Street. WMDs, 45 minutes, we all knew it was spin. They trampled over their own party and their own people to get their own way.'

'They?'

'We. I was there.'

'That's a heavy burden.'

She is relieved that Charlie doesn't try to excuse or justify.

'I resigned on the day of the invasion. I walked out and never went back.'

'All governments lie.'

'But I was part of this one.'

'New Labour—' Anger flares in Charlie's face. 'Hollow as a blown egg.'

'I know. I knew it long before Blair made his war pact with Bush, but—'

'What?'

'Eighteen years of the Tories. Any Labour government is better than that.'

'That's the argument the centrists always make.'

'And the left sell their souls and hope for the best.'

Charlie gives her a long look.

'Was that you?'

'Yes.'

'But you stopped hoping?'

The moon goes behind a cloud, throwing the terrace into shadow. In the dark she can voice the question that scares her the most.

'Why hope if it's all for nothing?'

Charlie answers without hesitation.

'Oh, my dear,' she says, 'hope is never nothing. It's everything.'

*

They are sitting on their bench on the Common. Charlie is eighteen again. It doesn't seem odd at all. The sun is shining, and the breeze is warm in her hair. She wants to lie against him, close her eyes and drift into sleep, but she can't. That isn't why she's here.

'Another war.'

Harry's head is thrown back, gazing at the sky.

'Where this time?'

'Iraq.'

'Why?'

'The usual reasons.'

He sits up, brushing a strand of dark hair from his eyes.

'Is it ever worth it?' she asks him.

'My war was.'

'You lost.'

'That changes nothing.'

'How can you say that?'

He reaches for her and pulls her into a kiss. The tears she has been holding back are wet on her cheeks and salty on both their tongues. She holds onto him, fierce and frightened. When she wakes up, it takes a few seconds before she realises that the old hand on the pillow, next to her face, is her own.

*

Margaret is standing at the edge of the shingle beach, where it meets the terrace. Behind her, Charlie comes out of the house with a jug of iced tea and a bowl of purple kalamata olives. She installs herself in her favourite chair with a sigh of contentment.

'Sunset,' she says. 'My favourite time of day. Golden light and the anticipation of a good dinner.'

Margaret smiles at her.

18

'David says there are two types of people—those who eat to live and those who live to eat.'

'And which is he?'

'Oh, definitely the latter.'

'I like the sound of him,' Charlie looks up, chewing an olive. 'How did you meet?'

'Work. He's a journalist too.'

'In the Press Office?'

'Oh no. He wouldn't be seen dead there. He's much wiser than I am.'

I was seduced by possibilities, wilfully blind. But he wasn't fooled. He quoted Maya Angelou to me. 'When someone shows you who they are, believe them the first time.'

'So where?'

'On a local paper back home. Years ago.'

'How many years?'

'Sixteen.'

'That's much better than I ever did. I was a serial monogamist.'

'Exciting!'

Charlie laughs. 'It was, at times. Tell me more about David.'

'What about you and your chain of affairs? Far more exciting.'

'Why didn't he come with you?'

Margaret's smile fades. She closes her eyes against the low sun, red dots behind her eyelids. Unbidden, his face rises up, wounded and questioning. She blinks him away, kicking at the stones beneath her feet, like a moody adolescent.

'I didn't ask him.'

'Ah.'

'It isn't his fault. None of it is.' She straightens up, feeling a sudden urge to apologise, to explain. 'I'm sorry.'

'For what?'

'I'm all over the place. It isn't just politics. Everything is a mess.'

She joins Charlie at the table, accepts a misty glass of amber tea, clinking with ice.

'Sweet tea and salty olives,' Charlie smiles. 'Delicious. We don't have to talk about it, my dear.'

'No. I want to.'

'Bewildered eyes.'

'What?'

'That's what I saw, that first night in the taverna. A strong woman. Independent. Abroad alone. And it was all betrayed by bewildered eyes.'

Margaret shakes her head, with a wry little smile.

'And I thought I was carrying it off so well.'

'Not so much.'

'It's like I'm living another life in my head. Looking at myself, remembering things I thought long forgotten. I was thinking this morning about when I was at school. The building was an ugly concrete block and I'd go about my day quite normally, but in my mind, I was at some Enid Blyton boarding school—all old stone and ivy and mullioned windows.'

Charlie laughs.

'When I was sixteen, I went to the Yorkshire Moors to find Heathcliff.'

'Honestly?'

'Well I knew he wasn't actually there, but I wanted him to be.'

'I thought it was just me.'

'Oh no, my dear, I think it's universal. We all have an imagined image of ourselves, don't we? A narrative in our heads. Bringing that and our real lives together is the challenge.'

'Does it ever happen?'

'It can. And that's when we are at our happiest, I think.'

Margaret is staring down at the mosaic, where the tiles still show traces of the wine she spilt on them, faint colour in the grout between the tesserae, pink veins in the blue of the flowers and the green of the fish.

'The war would have happened anyway,' Charlie says, reading her thoughts.

'I know.'

'Could you have made a difference?'

'Only to myself.'

With a nod of understanding, Charlie reaches out and takes Margaret's hand, cradling it in her own with a mixture of affection and protection. They sit quietly together until Charlie's face lights up suddenly with an unbidden memory.

'I met Sylvia Pankhurst once.'

Margaret's eyes widen.

'When? How?'

'In the 30s there were a lot of women in the Labour Party who had been Suffragettes. I knew quite a few. Two who had been in jail with Sylvia, on hunger strike and force-fed. Mighty women. One of them was an actress called Daisy Daniels. What a character! She and Sylvia were close friends and I had tea with them both at Daisy's house, just before the war.'

'That's extraordinary. What was she like?'

'Small. Fervent. Tireless.'

'Wow. I'm starstruck.'

'So was I.'

'Why did you tell me that now?'

'I remembered something Daisy said. That, during the General Strike, when it became clear that the strikers could never win, she started to doubt that things would ever change. Her faith was shaken. Like yours. She told me it was Sylvia who kept her going.'

'How?'

'By telling her that our job is just to carry the torch and pass it on to the next generation. That's all we have to do.'

'All?'

'I know.' Charlie laughs her deep, hearty laugh. 'Easier said than done.'

Out at sea, the sun is setting in a perfect circle on the horizon, sending a path of red and gold across the water almost to their feet. Across the table, Charlie is sitting forward in her chair, small and spirited and bristling with life.

'If you turn your face against your true self, then they really have won.'

There is something irresistible in what she offers. For a second Margaret allows herself the fleeting hope that perhaps there is a way back. The words come out of hiding in a rush.

'There's something else. I'm pregnant.'

Charlie nods almost imperceptibly.

'Yes, my dear, I thought you might be.'

1910

THERE I am, right in the middle of 'Morning Promenade' and it's going down a treat. Frank and Fanny Fairchild, the double act before me, had nearly sent the crowd to sleep with their 'Duets from Italian Opera' but a bit of ankle has livened the place up no end and old Davenport, the Manager, is standing at the back looking nearly happy. I think I catch a smile under his bushy moustache which is a first in my experience. So I'm feeling pretty chipper as I twirl my parasol and wink at a couple of cheeky chaps in the front row.

And then I sneak a peek into the wings to see if old Arthur is ready for his cue. He does a drunk act and more often than not he isn't acting, so there's a good chance I'll have to fill till they find him sleeping it off somewhere. Tonight he's there though, which is good. What isn't so good is the two Rozzers standing either side of him, looking at me like a donkey looks at a carrot. My heart drops into my stomach but I keep singing.

> *Do you think my dress is a little bit—*
> *Just a little bit—well not too much of it?*
> *Though it shows my shape just a little bit,*
> *That's the little bit the boys admire.*

All the way through the last chorus, I'm assessing my chances. The Coppers are on the stage door side, so there's no hope of doing a runner. I'm considering jumping over the orchestra pit and legging it up the aisle to freedom when two more of the buggers appear next to Mr Davenport and one of them leans in and whispers to him. Old Dav isn't smiling now. I can see I'm cornered so I take my bow, blow a few dainty kisses to the gallery and walk off smiling.

As Albert's entrance music starts up and he staggers on, the Rozzers bar my way. There's a tall, young Constable and a red-faced Sergeant, too fat for his tunic. They look like a comedy duo off the flickers.

'Daisy Daniels?' Junior steps forward.

'That's me, Officer,' I smile sweetly.

He holds out a brick with a piece of paper tied round it.

'I believe this is yours.'

'Somebody smashed a window in the Town Hall this morning,' says his mate. He unwraps the note and reads it out. 'Dear Prime Minister, Women would really like The Vote.'

'And we've got a witness. He swears it was you.'

I look 'em full in the eye and I don't even blink.

'He's got it wrong,' I say.

'He told us he's seen you on the stage. No mistaking you.'

'And he's ready to pick you out of a line-up.'

Fuck. I'm still smiling but I know the game's up now. Oh well, I knew when I chucked the bleedin' brick that it might come to this. So what? If they must have damage, then damage they shall have.

'The price of fame, eh?' I say as they lead me away.

So I bet you're asking how did a Music Hall nobody like me come to be agitating for the vote? It ain't a long story. You can't grow up in the East End, scratching a living among all the other desperate buggers, without feeling there has to be a better world to aim at. I'd been waiting all my life for something to fight for and I knew this was it as soon as I saw it.

Last year I was on the circuit with Hamilton's Diamond Review. It was our last day at The Hippodrome in Manchester and I was out for a breath of air between shows when I saw a crowd gathered in a little square behind the main street.

There was a gang of blokes laughing and yelling 'Good old Churchill' and 'Get back to the kitchen!'. One of 'em was clanging a hand bell. As I got closer I saw that they were chucking stuff—old veg and hunks of bread, any old rubbish they could lay their hands on. I worked my way round the side till I could see what they were aiming at. In the middle of the mayhem was a small group of women with a banner— a picture of a girl with a sword and a bugle; her hair was flowing in the wind and she was holding out her arms, like an invitation. I couldn't take my eyes off it.

A young woman was talking. I could hardly hear her with all the racket so I edged through the crowd till I came out right in front of her. She was tall and dark-haired. Her face wasn't pretty but it was strong and lively. She had a bruise on her cheek where something heavy had caught her, there were stains on her coat and tomato seeds in her hair, but she stood there like a rock and kept talking.

'I'm going to speak to you, so throw whatever you like. Go and fetch more if you want but I'm stopping here.'

She was wearing a sash in green, white and purple—the Suffragette colours. I'd seen women wearing 'em back in London, posh women in their beautiful coats and big hats. But this was different. This girl was ordinary. She was like me.

'Working people need the vote.'

'I know what you need!' came a shout from the back.

There was a lot of laughing and jeering and another shower of rubbish. I noticed a few Coppers at the edge of the square and thought they might step in to protect her. More fool me. They just stood with their hands in their pockets, grinning at each other.

'Not just women,' she carried on. 'Men like you lot. Why should the country be run by the rich for the rich? If I have to abide by the law then I want a say in the making of it, don't you?'

It was clear as day that she believed things could change. It was written in every line of her. And, watching her, I believed it too. I saw a different future. It was like my whole life was just leading up to that moment, like a light had been switched on in my head—and in my heart. I could have stayed there all day listening to her. But then I heard a church clock striking six and realised I had to run or I'd be late for the curtain. One of the women with her was holding a wad of leaflets. I asked her for one and I clutched it in my hand all the way back to the theatre, like a lucky piece.

After the show I went along to Henry's dressing room. He goes as Professor Miracle, the Memory Man and even though he tops the bill, there's no side to him. I tapped and popped my head round the door and he smiled and waved me in. Number One dressing rooms are a lot fancier than the shitholes I usually find myself in. This one had carpet and an armchair in front of a lovely big fire. I sat in it, toasting my toes, whilst Henry finished taking his make-up off. He was eating a pork pie and he gave me a piece. Chewing it, I took the leaflet out of my pocket and stared at it. Lines of black shapes that might as well have been secret code, for all they meant to me.

'What does it say, Henry?' I handed it over.

He ain't a real professor but he should be, the brains on him.

'Women have been asking for the vote for sixty years,' he read. 'They've been asking politely in drawing rooms and it's got them nowhere. Working people don't have the time for that. We won't wait any longer.'

I swallowed the last of my pie and gave him a long look.

'What do you think of it?'

'What do you think, Daisy? That's what matters.'

What did I think? I thought my birthday and Christmas had all come at once. These women felt like I did. They saw the wrong being done and burned to do something about it.

'I've found my calling,' I told him, and I couldn't wipe the smile off my face.

He looked thoughtful as he handed back the leaflet.

'You should be able to read this stuff for yourself,' he said. 'There's plenty you should be reading.'

'I never went to school.'

'Well, we've got another six months on the road. How about I teach you?'

And the rest, as they say, is history.

Some you win, some you lose. I get off with a caution for throwing the brick as it's a first offence. First time I've been caught, more like, though I don't enlighten 'em. But Old Davenport gives me the sack for 'bringing his theatre into disrepute'. Don't make me laugh. He's known for having the raciest shows in East London. Last week a group from the Methodist Mission fell to their knees in the stalls praying for God to lead us all to decency! Now I don't mind a bit of naughty—they don't pay sixpence to watch the Sally Army—but he's got a brass neck to talk about right and wrong with a theatre full of half-naked girls and lecherous punters.

'Woman's Right Wrongs No Man!' I yell as I bang the stage door behind me.

Outside, I stand for a minute, taking stock. Out of work. Fuck. Rent and food don't come for free so I need another job sharpish. I straighten my hat and make my way to Poverty Corner, on York Road, where the agents' offices are and where the acts hang about, hoping for good news.

There's a fair old crowd waiting when I get there, spilling out of the York Hotel onto the pavement. The Sinclair Brothers, Gentlemen Acrobats, are swinging round a streetlamp, trying to impress Little Maisie Bell, but she's seen it all before. Billy Collins is there, in his bright check suit and bowler. He's an institution, worked with Dan Leno for years, raking it in, riding high. He could make a stuffed bird laugh could Billy. These days he's half-cut by breakfast and pissed by dinner time.

'Alright, Daisy.'

The Winsome Twins are leaning either side of a doorway just behind me. Two peas in a pod. Blonde curls, blue eyes, rosebud lips, the whole package. I reckon they could make a decent living just standing still and being looked at but, truth is, they sing like angels. We shared digs for a Summer Season in Brighton a few years back. Six months and I still can't tell one from the other. Whether it was Lilly or Milly gave me a shout, your guess is as good as mine.

'You out of work? Thought you were at The Metropolitan?' Right hand twin.

'Davenport gave me the elbow. I got caught breaking windows.'

'You and your Votes for Women.' Left hand twin.

'Still, it's a bleedin' shame.'

'Thanks Milly,' I take a punt.

'I'm Lilly.'

'Sorry.' At least I know now. Till next time.

'Why do you do it?' asks Milly.

'The question is, why don't you?'

'Watch it Sis,' laughs Lilly, 'she's trying to recruit you.'

'Too right I am. You happy to be second class citizens?'

'It's the way of the world. It'll never change.'

'Well it won't for sure with that attitude. You think them in power'll just give it away, out of the goodness of their hearts? We have to fight for it. That's the lesson of history.'

I'm all set to give 'em the full benefit of my wisdom when

the door they're framing so prettily opens and out comes Gus Parker, assistant to Henry Mason, who runs half a dozen Halls south of the river. He's a self-satisfied little weasel of a man and I can't abide him but Milly and Lilly know which side their bread's buttered. They turn on their best dazzling smiles and he preens like a peacock.

'Mr Mason needs two acts for Wandsworth and one for Lewisham.'

No sooner has he said it than he's surrounded by hopefuls, clamouring for his attention. I consider walking away but pride doesn't fill your stomach, so I turn on the charm and give him a wink. I can't compete with The Winsome Twins but I know how to use what I've got and it works more than it doesn't, if I do say so myself.

Gus gives me an oily smile. 'Been a while, Daisy.'

'I've had a good run. Been busy.'

The smile stays on his face but his eyes go hard.

'Busy breaking windows, I hear.'

'Only between shows, Gus. Don't worry.'

'Oh I'm not worried. I've got a job, thanks. Don't fancy your chances of getting one though. You can shove off.'

The twins look uncomfortable, some of the crowd laugh but Jimmy the Juggler, who's standing behind me, steps up on the kerb and squeezes my arm, bless him.

'No need for that, Gus,' he says quietly.

'Mr Mason don't want no troublemakers in his Halls.'

'Well that's your call, but can't you be civil about it?'

'I'm not the one chucking bricks, am I?'

Gus has a look on his face that I see a lot. He's actually offended at the thought of Suffragettes, like he's threatened, like he has to protect his territory or something. It would be hilarious if it wasn't so bleedin' sad. He ain't got the vote neither. He ain't rich enough. Gus Parker needs to start questioning what he reads in the papers. Till then, he can take a long walk off a short pier and stick his fuckin' job.

'Thanks, Jimmy,' I say, 'but you're wasting your breath with Gus 'ere. He don't do decent. It's not in his nature.'

I wave at the twins, give Jimmy a smile and walk off with my head held high. I've got three bob in my purse and the rent's due on Sunday. Something better turn up soon.

I'm a glass half-full kind of person, me. Don't know why, when all's considered, but I am and I'm glad of it. Having said that, it's a blistering day and Bow is bleedin' awful in hot weather. It's no bed of roses at any time, with the soot and grime and the constant racket from the costers' barrows on every corner, but, in the heat, the stink from the soapworks knocks you sideways. It seeps through the bricks and up the stairwells and my room is putrid with it.

I'm renting an attic at the top of an old house near the church. The limewash on the walls is peeling and the tiny window under the sloping roof doesn't let much light in, but I've scrubbed it clean and there's a big brass bed, a cupboard for my bits and pieces and a shelf for my books. It's not bad. In this heatwave though, it's a choice between sweltering with the window closed or gagging at the stench with it open. So, though it's early for tonight's meeting, I go out anyway and make my way to the Public Hall.

It's open when I get there, but I'm the first to arrive. The chairs are set out in rows in front of the platform and I walk to the front and sit right in the middle. And then I wait. The sweat is running down my back under my stays, but it's dim and quiet in the big empty room and I sit still and think about the meeting. It's a special one tonight. Sylvia is speaking to us. Most Suffragettes worship her sister; they say that if all the world was on one side and Christabel Pankhurst on the other, they would go to her. Well, that's how I feel about Sylvia. She's plainer and quieter, she doesn't look for glory, but she works for the poor and powerless, every breathing moment. She's a diamond.

'Alright, Daisy?'

I open my eyes and blow me, if it ain't the Winsome Twins walking through the door.

'Thought we'd see what all the fuss is about,' says one of them as they waft down to the front and sit either side of me.

The other one leans in and squeezes my arm.

'Gus Parker was out of order today. Bastard.'

I stare at her in surprise.

'Is that why you're here?'

'It was Milly's idea. Us girls have got to stick together.'

They both smile and I get a little lump in my throat but I swallow it sharpish. Getting sentimental in my old age.

The room fills up quickly, mostly working women straight from a twelve-hour shift, bone-tired but with something like hope in their pinched faces. Milly and Lilly and me, we have it easy compared to the lives they lead. Suddenly there's a hush and there she is, walking onto the platform, a small figure in a simple grey dress and no hat. She doesn't look much. The twins look disappointed. But then she starts to talk.

'Friends,' she says, 'sisters. Today I met a fifteen-year-old girl who lives alone in a dismal room in Bethnal Green. The broken window is held together with putty, there are gaping holes in the floor and ceiling. No water, no heat, the only furniture a wooden chair and a threadbare mattress. She pays six shillings a week for this hovel. Her wage for fifteen hours a day washing dishes in a West End restaurant is seven shillings a week. She is starving whilst her landlord grows fat. She told me, "it's hard to keep straight". How many young girls lose that fight every day?'

I look at Milly and Lilly. She's got their attention. We've known more than a few who ended up on their backs to put food in their bellies.

'Friends,' says Sylvia. 'Nothing will change until the people have the power to bring change about. There are those who say that the working classes have nothing to offer in the fight for jus-tice—that their lives are too hard, their education too meagre to equip them for the struggle. I believe otherwise.'

I know what she's talking about. She's estranged from her family because of her work in the East End. Her mother and sis-ter aren't interested in the poor. Never mind 'Votes for Women', they should be shouting 'Votes for Toffs' cos that's all they're fighting for. Sylvia's worth ten of 'em.

'As of today, our movement has a thousand members in North Bow alone. It's the same all over the East End. I believe in this flame of enthusiasm. I believe with every fibre of my being that the rising of the masses is what will win this fight against enti-tlement and oppression.'

Applause bursts out all over the room. I jump up, cheering like mad. Either side of me, the twins get to their feet and join in. It's hard not to be convinced by Sylvia.

'Sisters—in the hall upstairs, the Mayor is addressing the Council. A room full of men making decisions about your lives and giving you no say in them. I urge you now to climb the stairs and let the men in power know the strength of your resistance!'

There's a surge for the doors. Shouts and laughter. Bags of flour are passed around and penny whistles. I look at the twins.

'You up for it?'

'With knobs on!'

We run up the stairs and burst into the meeting. The councillors don't know what's hit 'em!

'Votes for Women!' we yell at the top of our voices.

The Mayor is frozen to his chair behind the top table, red-faced and outraged.

'What are women coming to?'

'Their senses,' says Sylvia and up goes a cheer.

A few of the blokes try to grab us but they're outnumbered. Chairs and tables go flying. Clouds of flour, whistles shrieking, ink pots overturned and ripped agenda papers whirling like confetti. In the end, they run for it, the Mayor scuttling out in front, holding up his robes.

'We'll have the police on you!' he wails as he disappears down the corridor. One of the girls starts off 'The March of the Women' and we all join in.

Shout, shout, up with your song,
Cry with the wind for the dawn is breaking.
March, march, swing you along,
Wide blows our banner and hope is waking.

Laughing and singing, we pile down the stairs. Milly and Lilly are close behind me, a bit rumpled and floury but pink with excitement and sporting identical grins as we tumble onto the street.

'Time to make yourselves scarce, girls. Before the Old Bill gets 'ere.'

'What a lark!'

'When can we do it again?'

'Soon as you like. But better clear off now.'

Before they go, one of them catches my arm.

'That Sylvia Pankhurst,' her face is suddenly serious, 'she's something ain't she?'

'Yes,' I say. 'She truly is.'

The three bob in my purse has dwindled to tuppence and the rent's well overdue on my digs. Breakfast is the end of a three-day-old loaf and a cup of black tea. Still hungry, I scurry downstairs with one eye out for the landlord. I won't be able to dodge him much longer and then what? It's York Road again for me today and fingers crossed.

I'm passing Waterloo when I hear my name being called and there's my old mate Humph getting out of a cab. Humphrey Carter and his Celebrated Dogs have been top of the bill at the Bermondsey Star for months now and, by the look of him, he's raking it in. New suit, fancy watch chain, gold signet ring on his finger, he's looking well fed and happy as he waves me over.

'How's it going?'

'I'm alright, Humph,' I lie, more from habit than anything.

He gives me a look that tells me he isn't fooled. We know each other too well for that. A couple of years ago we had a little romance—he's easy on the eye is Humph. It didn't last long; a few walks, a few suppers, a bit of slap and tickle and then he was off on tour and neither of us was heartbroken.

'You hungry?' he asks.

I think about denying it but what's the point? I could eat a scabby donkey and he knows it. Ten minutes later we've got a booth in the White Lion, I'm happily working my way through a beef and oyster pie and he's twinkling at me across the table.

'Don't you get any ideas,' I tell him between bites. 'I owe you lunch. No extras.'

He throws back his head and laughs.

'You don't change, Daisy Daniels.'

'What you see is what you get.'

'Wouldn't have it any other way.' He points at my jacket lapel where my Suffragette brooch is pinned. 'You're not hiding it then?'

'Why should I?'

I'm proud to wear it. A little circle of green enamel with Votes for Women and WFL in gold letters. The Women's' Freedom League. People think it's all about the Pankhursts in this game but there are lots of groups in the fight and I've no time for Christabel and her mother. Since I learned to read, I know the words for what I feel and think. I'm a Socialist. A Radical. Everything Mrs Pankhurst despises. The WFL is for those who know that Votes for Women is just the start.

'Look here, Daisy,' suddenly Humph is serious, 'I'm not boasting but I can pull strings these days. I can get you a job but only if you stop this suffrage lark. It ain't popular.'

I've got a lovely piece of beef halfway to my mouth but it doesn't get there. I put my knife and fork down and glare at him.

'Is that right?'

'Now don't get narky with me. I don't care how many windows you smash but other people do. It goes against you. You know it does. Just take off those colours and I'll get you booked up for the year. It's no more than you deserve.'

It's tempting, course it is. I'm tuppence away from the workhouse and I'm scared. My digs are nothing to write home about, but I lie awake at night, terrified at the thought of not having 'em to come back to. Course I want a bleeedin' job. But I can't do it. I just can't.

'Thanks, Humph,' I say, 'but it's too late to take 'em off now.'

He can see it's a waste of time. He shakes his head at me.

'Eat your pie. It's getting cold.'

I get back to my meal. Fuck knows where the next one is coming from.

Then Humph sits forward.

'Right. How about this? The dogs need taking out once a day—a good run in the park or they get fretful. They know you well enough. I'll pay you to take the job off my hands till you've got something better to do.'

It takes a minute to register. Then I'm so relieved that, for a minute, everything goes swimmy. That lump in my throat is back and I swallow it down with the last bit of pie. When I can focus again, he's just sitting there, looking at me, waiting.

'You're just inventing a job to help me.'

'That's right.'

'It's a loan.'

'Don't worry.'

'No.'

'Alright, girl. Whatever you like.'

He smiles at me. He's got a lovely, cheeky smile that can't help but lift your heart, however bad things are.

'You're a good bloke.'
'I'm a bleedin' saint, that's what I am.'
'I'll pay you back first chance I get.'
'Alright then.'
'Right then.'

The dogs are kennelled in the yard behind the theatre. The main doors are open so I take a short cut through front of house to the pass door. The Star is pretty fancy, I must say. Plush seats, red walls and a gilded ceiling. A lovely little gallery too, decorated with wrought-iron work, all filigree leaves and flowers. The tabs are drawn so I can't see the stage but the arch is tall and wide, crammed with plaster nymphs and naked-arsed cherubs smiling down on the orchestra pit. All very lah-di-dah. Till you get backstage, of course, then it's bare walls, floorboards, peeling plaster and mousetraps in every corner. There are two dressing rooms. Gents and Ladies. I have a little sit in front of a mirror and breathe in the smell of greasepaint. Moving from digs to digs and town to town, nowhere is home to me and a theatre is the nearest I get to feeling like I belong.

'What's going on 'ere?'

An ancient, stooped old man is standing in the doorway, looking at me through watery eyes.

'You Ned?' I ask him.

'That's right.'

'I've come to walk Humphrey's dogs. He says you'll have the keys.'

He walks closer, peering into my face.

'I know you. You're Daisy Daniels. I saw you in panto at the Astoria. You made a lovely Fairy.'

'Thanks. I do my best.'

He hands me a set of keys and nods towards a door at the end of the corridor. Then he shuffles off. Humph says Ned has been stage door keeper at The Star for nigh on fifty years. I can believe it, looking at him.

As soon as I get outside the dogs start yelping. Blimey, four Jack Russells can make a right ol' din when they get going.

'Alright. Keep it down.'

Maybe they recognise my scent. They jump up against the wire mesh, ears up, tails wagging. The cage is roomy and weatherproof and there's food and blankets in there but they want out, that's for sure.

'Hello, lads. It's me, Daisy. Time for walkies.'

Their leads are hanging on named hooks. Matthew, Mark, Luke and John. Humph's idea of a joke.

'Right. Sit.'

They drop onto their haunches in a perfect row. The Celebrated Dogs are trained to within an inch of their lives. On stage they pirouette on two legs, jump through burning hoops and play 'God Save the King' on the tubular bells twice nightly. Taking 'em out is a walk in the park, in every sense of the word. I owe Humph and I won't forget it.

Southwark Park is busy with people making the most of the good weather. The lake is full of little boats and a string quartet is playing in the bandstand. I take the dogs to a stretch of empty grass and let them off the leash, so they can have a run. There's a young woman sitting on a bench in the shade of a big tree. She's having a baby. Her belly is huge. Her clothes are tidy but cheap and old. They're out of season too and she looks hot and uncomfortable, but she gives me a smile as I sit down.

'What a scorcher!'

Close up, she's pale and tired. Big dark circles under her eyes. And she's very young. Just a kid. I wonder who's looking after her. She's wearing a wedding ring but what does that guarantee?

'Do you live round 'ere?' I ask her.

'Not far. But I work down there on Slippers Place.' She nods to a long, low terrace behind the trees. 'I'm on my break.'

'You're still working? When is it due?'

'A few weeks.'

'Bloody hell!'

'It's only sewing. We need the money.'

Course they do. She'll be working for peanuts too and every penny spent before it's earned.

'Is that a Suffragette badge?' She's looking at my jacket.

'Yes.'

'Votes for Women?'

'Not just votes. Equality. Respect. Education. Our fair share of everything.'

'Sounds lovely.'

'It will be.'

She's polite. She doesn't contradict me. But nothing in her face is anything like hope. Making people believe that the world can't change is the enemy's greatest success. Religion and the newspapers keeping everyone in their place and all's right with the world. Well it isn't. Change is coming, you mark my words.

'It was nice talking to you.'

She stands up, hand in the small of her back, and walks away, heavy-footed, across the grass. I call the dogs and they come running, eyes bright, tongues lolling, panting for breath. As I fix their leads I watch her awkward gait and think of my mum, at sixteen, walking to the workhouse with me in her belly, and never walking out.

I looked her up after I'd learned to read. Kitty Daniels, orphan and widow. Born County Cork, 1868, died Well Street Workhouse, 1884. She left nothing. I've no idea what she looked like. Sometimes I look in the mirror and wonder if I get my eyes from her or my hair. Never saw my dad either. My birth record says he was a soldier killed in Africa. Private Elijah Daniels, aged twenty-two. I tried to find his family but they all died of typhus fever before I was born. I'm twenty-eight and I've lived longer than any of 'em. The poor rest lightly on the world.

*

I take enough from Humph to pay my rent and eat cheap and I pawn everything I've got, which ain't much. The heatwave passes and when I'm not at Poverty Corner or walking the dogs, I sit on my bed, reading stuff I've borrowed from the WFL. There's so much to learn and I started late, so I'm making up for lost time. I love it. The whole wide world is in books.

Then, at long bleedin' last, I get lucky. Mary O'Connell, 'Ireland's Gem', does a runner to America with her Fenian sweetheart and Forester's Music Hall needs a quick replacement for 'The Emerald Isle'. I'm down there as soon as I hear about it, front of the queue. A dead Irish mother, red hair and a few verses of 'The Kerry Dancing' does the trick and hally-bloody-looyah I'm in work again. Forester's is a bit of a dive but it pays enough to get my stuff out of hock and make a little dent in what

I owe Humph. We have words about me paying him back but I put my foot down.

'If you don't take it, we'll fall out.'

'Alright, girl,' he says. 'The dogs will miss you.'

'I'll come visit.'

'Make sure you do.'

I get the job Monday, and Tuesday I'm on. I've learnt half a dozen Irish ballads in a hurry and the lyrics are pretty similar, so I have a few mishaps, but on the whole, I get away with it. The crowd are rougher than I've had for a while. A lot of drunks and a few girls open for business, if I'm not mistaken. I can't help thinking about The Star and its plush and gilt whilst I'm looking out at the faded drapes and the wooden benches in the gallery, but beggars can't be choosers, can they?

I've just started the last chorus of 'The Rose of Tralee' when I notice a bloke on his own in one of the stage boxes. He's wearing white tie and a silk topper and has a shiny, well-fed look about him. Quite a few toffs come slumming it to the Music Hall when the mood takes 'em. This one sits up and takes notice when I come on and what he's thinking is written all over his face.

She was lovely and fair, as the rose of the summer
But 'twas not her beauty alone that won me.

I can feel his eyes on me every second. He'd never look at one of his own like that but we don't get the same consideration. I don't give him any attention, just keep singing.

Oh no, 'twas the truth in her eye ever dawning,
That made me love Mary, the Rose of Tralee.

I take my bow and walk off. That's me done and I've got a late-night meeting to go to, a special one. Sylvia Pankhurst is in hiding from the law, but she's breaking cover tonight to speak to us. We've been planning it for days, all very hush hush, so all I'm thinking about is getting there. Big mistake to drop my guard. I come out into the back alley and there he is.

It's a rainy night, a thin drizzle like mist in the light of the street lamp at the corner and greasy on the cobbles by the stage door. He's got a fancy evening cape keeping him dry but I'm not so fortunate. I've no intention of hanging about anyway. I turn towards the main street but he moves quickly and blocks my way.

'Scuse me,' I say, politely enough. 'Can I get by?'

'Hello, Daisy.'

He's youngish, tall and broad shouldered. Probably played rugby at his fancy school. He looks strong which ain't good.

'I'm in a hurry.'

I push past him but he grabs me.

'That isn't very friendly, is it?'

He has a posh accent—no surprise—and a smile that has nothing pleasant about it.

'You're no friend of mine.'

I struggle but it's no good. He pulls me further up the alley into the dark.

'What's your price, Daisy?'

'Get off me!'

He just laughs and pushes me against the wall. He smells of hair oil and brandy. Fuck. I should never have come out alone.

'Little wildcat, aren't you?'

'Piss off!'

He tries to kiss me. I squirm away and the stubble on his chin scrapes my cheek like sandpaper. I lash out and land a punch and he's not laughing any more. His face is twisted and ugly.

'You whore. You dirty whore.'

He forces me to my knees. His flies are already unbuttoned. The bastard was prepared. Proper bleedin' boy scout. He grabs my hair and pushes his crotch into my face. I'm panicking. My heart is pounding. No way is he getting what he wants from me. No bleedin' way. And then I remember Bobby Henderson and the story he told me one night, after a few too many snifters in The Rose and Crown, and my mind clears.

'You'll be sorry,' I tell him.

'Open your mouth, bitch.'

I do as he says. He groans. His legs tremble against me. And then I close my teeth on him and bite down hard and he screams like a stuck pig.

I pull away and scramble to my feet. He's bent double, still howling. I taste his blood in my mouth and my stomach rises. Retching and shaking, I leg it down the alley to the light and noise and the late-night crowds. I'm wet through and muddy and my hair is a wild mess. A woman selling hot potatoes asks me if I'm alright.

'Had a spot of bother.'

'Shall I shout for a Copper?'

She looks down the alley behind me, putting two and two together.

'He's a toff,' I say.

She gets what I'm saying. My word against his. She gives a nod and hands me a little bag of spuds.

'On the house,' she says.

I thank her. The bag is warm and I realise how cold I am. I think about going home for a bit. Eat my potatoes, read a book, pull myself together. But I don't want to miss the meeting. I promised Milly and Lilly I'd see them there and I want to hear Sylvia. So I take a few deep breaths to steady myself and then I make my way to Bow Baths where it's all happening. As I walk through the rain, I think about Bobby, the little Mary who sings sweet tenor in a Barbershop quartet and gets set upon regular because of how he's made. That night in the pub, he told me the biting trick saved his bacon many a time. I owe him one. It'll be a while before that bastard in the alley has a piss without yelling.

When I get there, I go round the back, as planned. The building is closed for the winter but one of the girls is walking out with the caretaker and he's opening up for us in secret tonight. There's a crowd of women standing in the dark, hushed and waiting. A door opens and in we go, silent till we're safe inside. With the windows covered, we light the lamps and breathe a bit easier. I see the twins and give them a wave.

'Bleedin' hell, what happened to you?'

I've had a go at tidying myself up, but I still look like I've been dragged through a hedge backwards.

'Punter got a bit amorous.'

They understand. We've all been there one way or another. It goes with the territory.

'You alright?'

'Yeah.' In spite of myself I feel the tears starting to well up.

'Oh, Daisy—'

'Bastard.'

'It's nothing,' I say. 'I got away.'

There's a young woman standing behind them, close enough to get the gist of the conversation and she gives me a sympathetic look. She's not a regular but there's something familiar about her. I can't put my finger on it at first and then it dawns on me. It's the girl who kept talking, whatever was chucked at her, who opened my eyes and changed my life.

'You're from Manchester, aren't you?' I ask her.

'Aye.'

'I saw you speak. You're the reason I joined the movement.'

She looks surprised.

'Is that right?'

'True as I'm standing here.'

She has one of those smiles that lights up her whole face, softens it. She steps towards me and holds out a hand.

'I'm Nora.'

'Daisy,' I say. 'Pleased to meet you.'

'Likewise.'

'You're a long way from home.'

'There's a few of us down from Salford to hear Sylvia.'

'She comes from near you, doesn't she?'

'Aye. But she doesn't get back too often these days.'

'So the mountain has come to Mahomet?'

She laughed.

'It's worth it.'

There's a bustle of activity and in comes Sylvia, disguised in old clothes and a big battered hat. We're turning to greet her, congratulating ourselves on our cleverness, when the door opens again and a dozen Coppers push through, with the caretaker behind 'em, smirking. The bastard must have dobbed us in. His poor sweetheart looks mortified. She crosses to him and slaps him hard across the face. The rest of us are about to set on him like a pack of hounds when the Coppers make a grab for Sylvia, so we have bigger fish to fry. We've got her surrounded in seconds and they can't get at her.

All they can see is her hat in the crowd. Nora is tall enough to reach over and grab it. In a second, she swaps it for her own and, taking her cue, someone else does the same then someone else, till it's going round in circles and the Rozzers have no idea which one of us is the one they want.

That's when they start to throw their weight about in earnest, lashing out with their night-sticks at whoever's in their way. The girl next to me is knocked unconscious and drops to the floor like a stone. I try to pull her out of the scrum before she gets trampled but I can't get a grip on her through the forest of legs and I'm going down myself when four hands grab me and the twins pull me upright.

'Thanks, girls.'

'Welcome.'

'Help me move her,' I say, but before we can do anything, a Copper hits one of them on the shoulder with such force that his truncheon flies out of his hand. I hear a sickening crack and a scream.

'Milly!' Her sister runs to her.

'I think he's broken something.' She's as white as a ghost, holding her arm and whimpering in pain.

'Get her out of here,' I tell Lilly.

'That bastard—'

'I'll sort it.'

All in all, it's been quite a night and I've had as much as I can take. I make a dive for the stick and whirl it round my head, cursing like a demon. I see the twins slip out of the door as the Copper comes at me, then I thwack him as hard as I can and keep beating him till he wrestles it from my hand. He'll have some bruises in the morning and I'm glad he will. Fucker. And fuck the government that encourages them to knock us about. If they think they can beat us into submission, they can think again.

But that's how I end up in Holloway.

We're sent down for ten days. There's six of us, including Nora and Sylvia. We know we have to kick up a fuss until they treat us as political prisoners—books and paper allowed, no prison dress, no solitary—but from the off it's clear that ain't happening. When they produce the uniforms with broad arrows painted on them, we link arms with our backs against the wall and refuse to undress. A crowd of wardresses appear and we're outnumbered three to one and dragged apart. They literally rip the clothes off us till we're standing shivering in our smalls. We look to Sylvia and she gives us the nod to put the uniforms on.

Mine's too big and none too clean. Then we're shoved, one at a time, into a bleak room where they fire questions at us. Name? Age? Occupation? Religion?

'I'm a political prisoner,' I say.

They take no notice. Up to now I've been angry, even enjoying it in a way, taking pride in the fight. But I'm not enjoying it any more. Holloway is a miserable, cold place with barred windows set into high stone walls and corridors echoing with footsteps and clanging doors. I think I can hear crying in the distance, a woman wailing, heartbroken. No point lying about it, I'm scared, but I try not to show it as I'm taken to my cell and locked in.

Left on my own, I sit on the low bed and give myself a little talking to. Pull yourself together, Daisy. Others have done it and so can you. This is the struggle. This is what it takes.

'Stay strong, sisters!'

It's Sylvia's voice ringing out. I can hear footsteps, doors closing, bolts being drawn.

'Votes for Women!' shouts Nora and a cheer goes up.

I run to the door and peer through the little grill. It's so dim I can't see a thing.

'Unity is strength!' I yell into the darkness. 'No Surrender!'

'Sing for us, Daisy,' says Sylvia as the voices die down. 'Sing "Shoulder to Shoulder".'

So I stand in my cell and sing my heart out.

Women young and older
Shoulder put to shoulder
In the might of sacred right
Bolder still and bolder.
Let no ancient custom blind you
Let one bond of suffering bind you
Leave unrighteous laws behind you,
Soon you shall be free!

When I finish, everything is quiet. If they're anything like me, the others are trying not to cry. Funny how alone you can feel, even when you know there are people close by. I give myself a shake and concentrate on having a proper look around me.

There's one tiny window high up by the ceiling, a shelf, a

stool, the plank bed and a bucket. On the shelf is a thin towel, a piece of hard, yellow soap, a Bible and a wooden spoon. Above it, a little lamp is set into the wall behind thick glass. That's the lot.

The bolts are drawn back and the door opens. A wardress puts an enamel bowl and cup on the stool in the corner. She doesn't speak, doesn't even look at me. She walks out and locks me in again. I go over and have a butcher's. It's some kind of stew. I'm hungry but I don't touch it. We don't eat in prison. It's part of the protest. I drink the water in the cup, drape my little towel over the bowl and go back to the bed.

I reckon it can't be far off eight o'clock. The second house will be kicking off at Forester's any time soon. I've never wished for anything as much as I wish I was there right now, singing for the drunks and the street girls.

It's a warm summer evening outside but the little patch of sky through the bars seems like another world and the cell has a clinging dankness that sets me shivering. I can smell the food and it's hard not to eat it. I try to read the Bible—me, reading the bleedin' Bible! I look for the bit that says we are all equal in the sight of God but I can't find it. I get undressed and, in just my shift, I lie under the rough blanket, teeth chattering, staring out into the shadows. Ten days. Seems like a lifetime.

'Goodnight friends,' Sylvia calls from somewhere in the darkness and we all join in.

'Quiet!' raps a voice from the corridor but we ignore it.

'This too shall pass.'

She's been through this before so she knows what she's talking about. The thought of it helps me find my courage and I curl up on my side and go to sleep.

*

I know what it's like to be hungry, the life I've led, but not like this. Nothing like this. My head is pounding, I feel sick and dizzy and the taste in my mouth is bleedin' awful. Sylvia says it's normal and that the hunger pangs stop after a few days. Mine haven't. I think about food all the time. I dream about it all night.

On the fourth day they start bringing lovely stuff in. Chicken broth, braised beef and mash, egg custard. They leave the dishes in the cell for ages. The smell is like a drug. It climbs inside me, hollows me out to screaming emptiness. I think I'll actually go stark, staring mad if I don't eat. Just one mouthful. How could that hurt? Just a taste. But I know it's no good. If I start eating, nothing on earth will make me stop. I feel like I'm dying and I'm more scared than I've ever been in my life.

I spend a lot of time leaning against the door, my ear to the little grill, listening to the girls calling to each other and joining in when I can. Sylvia talks about her father and what an inspiration he was to her. Keir Hardie too. She's very close to him. As close as it gets, if you ask me, but that's her business. She tells us how poor he was growing up and how he would take newspapers from dustbins for want of something to read.

Nora tells us about her great-gran who was transported to Australia and had her baby daughter torn from her arms at the quayside. That's what the system did to her. No wonder Nora wants to tear it down. Suddenly I'm raging. I'm weak and dizzy but I can't keep still. I have to do something. Anything. That's when I see the hole in the thin mattress on my bed. A few fibres of straw matting are poking out. I sit up and pull at it, work at it with busy fingers until I can get a handful of the stuff through the hole. I climb on the stool, grab my enamel mug off the shelf and hammer it against the glass in front of the lamp until it breaks. Twice I nearly pitch off, I'm so light-headed, but at last the glass shatters. I hold the straw to the flame and it smoulders. Blimey, it stinks! I drop it on the floor and get busy tearing pages out of the Bible to add to my little fire. When it's alight, I hold my pillow over it till it catches. In seconds there's a proper blaze, roaring like a furnace and the cell fills with smoke. I run to the door and hammer on it with the mug.

'Votes for Women! No Surrender!'

It's only then it dawns on me that I might have gone too far. If nobody comes I could be a goner in no time. It strikes me as funny and I start to laugh and once I start, I can't stop. I'm bent double, with tears streaming down my face, from the laughing and the smoke and I'm choking while I laugh, gasping for air and beating the door but nobody comes near. I can hear the girls in the other cells calling me but I can't answer. I can't breathe, never mind talk. Finally, I hear footsteps and the bolts being drawn but I don't see who it is because that's when the dark closes in.

I wake up in a padded cell. A proper loony-bin padded cell. I lie there looking up at the ceiling for a long time. Slowly I realise that I've been washed, my hair has been combed and I'm wearing a clean nightdress. I feel comfier than I have for days. And then I realise that I don't actually know what day it is or how long I've been out of it. Or whether I'm still in prison. Or if I've been put away in a nuthouse and forgotten about. That's when I jump up in a panic and look around for the door, but every surface is the same—dirty cream and cushioned – even the floor, which sinks under my bare feet as I walk the walls.

'Bloody hell, Daisy,' I tell myself, 'you've really done it this time, girl.'

Then I realise I'm talking to myself, giving anyone watching or listening even more proof that I'm off my rocker, so I shut up.

The door, I soon learn, is in the corner, cos it opens a few minutes later. I can't tell you how relieved I am to see one of the wardresses. Still in Holloway then.

'What happened to me?'

'You don't remember?' Her face is expressionless. 'You tried to burn the prison down.'

'I remember that. But then what?'

'You collapsed. Then the doctor gave you a sedative.'

'How long have I been out?'

'Just overnight.'

Shame. I was hoping it was longer and more of my sentence gone. She hands me a bundle of clothes.

'This way.'

I follow her back to the cells. She pushes a door open and I go in. A different room. Even smaller. The alcove in the wall is empty.

'No lamp?'

She isn't amused.

She closes the door, locks and bars it and I hear her footsteps fade away. I stand in the middle of the room in my nightdress and bare feet with my hair loose around my face and I feel like a kid again, a scared child, cold and helpless and alone. I run to the door and shout as loud as I can, though my throat is dry as dust.

44

'Who's around? Who can hear me?'

'I can.' It's Nora. She sounds a long way away. 'Are you alright Daisy?'

'Where's everyone else? Why can't I hear them?'

'They've put you in isolation. You're a bad influence.' She laughs. 'Good for you.'

The next day, I'm lying on my bed when I hear a new sound. Metal wheels on the stone floor of the corridor. It passes my door and moves on, with footsteps and the squeaking and grinding of whatever is being pushed. Then it stops. Bolts are drawn, a door opens and closes. A few minutes later, almighty hell breaks loose. Banging and crashing, shouts and yells. I push myself upright and stagger to the door. There's nothing to see through the grill. Everything goes quiet for a minute. Then screams. Awful, terrifying screams. Then silence.

'It's Sylvia.' Nora's voice is faint and cracked in the distance. 'Force-feeding.'

I don't remember sinking but I realise I'm on the floor, back to the wall and the cell is spinning like a carousel. I've seen women who've been force-fed, the state they're in when they come out, the horror stories they tell. I'm so scared I can't breathe.

I hear the locks and bolts again, the metallic scraping, more struggling, more screaming. And repeat. Then the footsteps stop at my door and my heart is beating out of my chest. I crawl on my hands and knees to the bed and grab onto it.

Two men and six women crowd into the cell. There's barely room for all of us in there. The noise I've been hearing is coming from a trolley on wheels. I can see some lengths of rubber tubing, funnels, a metal jug and a glass of milk. Something else too, small and steel. I don't know what it is but it scares me half to death. A wardress puts a chair in the middle of the room.

'Will you drink this milk, Daisy?' one of the men asks. He's tall with dark hair and a bushy beard. His manner is calm and business-like.

'Miss Daniels to you,' I croak.

'I'm Dr Graham. If you don't take nourishment now, you will be forcibly fed. Will you drink the milk?'

I can't stop shaking but amazingly, miraculously, I feel my

45

anger rising again. Blazing, bleedin' fury actually. How dare they treat us like this? How fucking dare they? I get to my feet and hold out a hand for the glass and they all look relieved as I take it. Then I throw the milk full in his face. I hardly have time to enjoy the sight of him dripping white before they're on me and I'm kicking and fighting and swearing like a docker whilst they force me into the chair.

One woman on each arm, two holding my legs down, two holding my shoulders back. They've got the routine off pat. Dr Graham's hands are on my jaw, pushing the steel thing into my mouth. It forces my teeth apart and holds them open. The sharp edges cut into my gums and I taste blood. The other doctor, who hasn't bothered to introduce himself, forces my head back and holds it like a vice. I'm still heaving and twisting but it's no good. Dr Graham rams the tube down my throat and it feels like it's ripping a hole in me. I'm choking and retching and screaming but he keeps pushing it down, down into my stomach. Then he picks up the jug and pours the liquid food through the funnel. I feel the chill of it in my throat and chest, like a violation. His beard is still wet with milk, I smell the carbolic soap on his hands, I feel the heat of my struggling body and the sweat soaking through my clothes. Everything hurts. Something wet falls on my clenched hand and I realise it's a tear, that the wardress holding down my right arm is crying silently, and I feel the pity, the awful wrong of it as the tube is pulled out and most of the food comes spewing back in a bitter flood.

My insides feel flayed, my eyes are streaming, I'm spitting blood and bile. The men don't even look at me as they push the trolley to the door. Two of the women help me to the bed and I fall on it like a bag of rags.

'We'll be back tomorrow if you don't eat before then,' says Dr Graham.

'Fuck off.'

The wardress who was crying covers me with the blanket. Her face is flushed with shame and she tries to meet my eyes but I'm in no mood for understanding. I turn my face to the wall, the door opens and closes and they're gone. In the sudden quiet, I think of the others lying weak and aching on their beds, covered in their own vomit, and I start to cry, like I haven't done since I was a kid, scared and lonely in the workhouse. What's the point of solidarity and sisterhood when the bastards can tear us apart and torture us in secret? Women have been going through this hell for years and who knows? Who cares? We could all die in here. I'm staring at the little window, up high in the wall and out of nowhere, a piece of poetry pops into my head.

I never saw a man who looked
With such a wistful eye
Upon that little tent of blue
Which prisoners call the sky.

Oscar Wilde. What did he do to deserve his sufferings? But the powers that be destroyed him anyway, the men in charge who do worse than we do every day, condemn the rest of us to poverty and powerlessness and never pay the price. They don't even think it's wrong. They believe they're entitled and we can't touch them. Churchill says he won't be hen-pecked into giving us the vote. Fuck him. Fuck 'em all. I pull myself upright, take my piece of hard soap and write on the wall beside me in great big letters—No Surrender. You can only see it now and then, when it catches the light, but I know it's there.

The forcible feeding carries on. My mouth is torn and swollen and my body dark with bruises. The wardress I saw crying doesn't cry anymore. I suppose you get used to everything in the end. They send a Home Office surgeon to listen to our hearts. If one of us dies in here, we'd give the movement a martyr. They can't have that.

On Sunday, they're holding me down in the chair when I hear singing. They're force-feeding us whilst the service is going on in the chapel, torturing women to the sound of 'Holy, Holy, Holy'. Afterwards, I come round to find the Chaplain sitting at my bedside. I tell him to fuck off.

How long is ten days? I stop calling to the others. Haven't got the voice. Or the energy. I've got the shakes though. And awful pain in my chest and shoulders. I'm not sure whether it's day or night, whether I'm awake or dreaming. Sometimes I feel like I'm floating down a warm river, sometimes I'm in the cold depths, fighting for breath. My head is full of screams and the terrible sound of the choking of women. I put my hands over my ears and it gets louder. The darkness behind my eyes flushes red as blood and I think, this is it, I've gone mad, I'm lost for ever.

When they bring my own clothes and shoes, I don't understand what's happening. They have to dress me in a chair cos I can't stand up. Outside in the corridor, leaning on two wardresses, I see Sylvia, Nora and the others helped out of their cells, as weak as me, and it starts to dawn on me that it's over. I don't know how I feel, whether to laugh or cry, and anyway I haven't got the strength to do either. We just look at each other, wide eyes in gaunt faces.

The corridor to the gates seems endless. Nora squeezes my arm and bends to whisper in my ear.

'One foot in front of the other.'

I pull myself upright and we walk side by side to freedom.

Outside, the sky is wide and bright. There's a cold wind blowing but it feels like heaven. A small crowd is waiting. Lots of cheering and flags waving. The noise is deafening. Faces are blurring. I think I'm seeing double then realise it's the twins running towards me, tears streaming. But I drop before they reach me and I'm confused cos the ground isn't hard, it's warm and comfy and smells lovely.

'I've got you, girl,' says Humph as my eyes close. 'I've got you.'

1915

THE new lass was in the laundry tent, trying to clean a uniform crusted with dried blood. No surprise she was getting nowhere, it was more blood than khaki. She didn't look up as I passed her, just kept dunking the brush in a bucket of soapy water and scrubbing away as if her life depended on it. Happen it did at that point—she had that lost look on her face.

'What's that you're doing?'

She didn't break rhythm, just kept dunking and scrubbing.

'They send the uniforms home with the personal effects.'

'We haven't time to clean 'em,' I said. 'There's too many.'

'Some mother or wife will open the parcel. It smells of death.'

Her hands started to shake. I went over and took hold of the brush.

'You can't wash the war away with a bar of soap.'

This one wouldn't last. I knew it when I first saw her this morning. I walked into my tent, bone tired after a twelve-hour shift and there she was in her shiny new uniform. I'd had the place to myself for a few weeks and quite liked it but that couldn't be helped. No, what really narked me was that she was reading Rupert Brooke. Rupert bloody Brooke.

'Don't tell me,' I said. 'He's why you've come.'

'He's an inspiration—'

'He's dead.'

I dropped onto my bunk. She looked at me like I'd slapped her. I know, I should have given her the welcome speech but I was too weary for the world-fit-for heroes stuff and, to be honest, her posh vowels put the tin lid on it.

'*Some corner of a foreign field that is forever England,*' I said.

'Yes.'

'Bloody hell.'

'What?'

'You'll learn.'

I turned over and went to sleep. This was the first I'd seen of her since.

'What I saw today,' her voice was shaking, 'it makes me pray all I know are killed outright.'

I've thought that myself, more than once. Not that I do any praying. We're sixty miles from the fighting here and, by the time they get to us, the wounds are days old, caked in sand, septic and flyblown. Blood, bone, pus, lice and maggots. Grown men screaming and crying for their mams. You never get used to it but at least you learn what to expect. You adapt. Or you break.

'You should go to the Red Cross tent,' I said. 'Get a brew.'

Hot, sweet tea. The British answer to everything. Even carnage.

She wiped her wet hands on her apron. Pale, soft hands. She's never done a proper day's work in her life.

'That poem of Brooke's. I felt like he was speaking directly to me.' She had that light in her eyes. Just like the women back home, handing out white feathers to lads who hadn't rushed into uniform. 'I couldn't sit at home in my mother's sewing circle or have tea at the vicarage as if nothing was happening, as if the fight for freedom was someone else's war.'

The fight for freedom. If I'd a penny for every time I've heard that. I was tempted to give her chapter and verse right there but I bit my tongue and settled for introductions.

'I never asked your name. Mine's Nora Barnes.'

'Rose. Rose Paget.'

'Welcome to Lemnos, Nurse Paget.' I nodded across at the tunic, dripping red onto the earth floor. 'Whose was it?'

'Corporal Miller's.'

'Little Billy? I thought he'd make it.'

'Haemorrhage.'

He'd shown me a picture of his sweetheart, said I reminded him of her. We get that a lot.

'He was always smiling,' I said. 'Even here.'

'He was a hero.'

'He was cannon fodder.'

Her eyes widened with shock. She took a step back then picked up the sodden tunic and walked out of the tent without another word. I've blotted my copybook with Nurse Paget, good

50

and proper, but I'm not sorry. She can dream all she likes about the glory of war but the least we owe poor Billy Miller is the truth.

*

The sunsets are beautiful here. Purple hills, lilac sea and the boats in the harbour silhouetted black against a pink sky. Drink it in, Nora, I tell myself. Drink it in and store it up against the horror inside those tents lining the shore. I don't know what the other girls do to survive but this has worked for me so far. Keep it safe, so when you close your eyes and the nightmare images start, you can call it up to paint over them, you can remember this moment's peace and be saved from madness.

It was scorching today. We put netting across the open ends of the tents to keep the flies out, but it didn't work. They love blood. Corporal Webb was burning with fever and begging for water but there's a shortage again. I gave him my ration. It didn't touch his thirst. I swapped his sweat-soaked pillow for a fresh one and changed the stinking black dressing on his leg. You never get used to the stench of gangrene, sickly-sweet and rotten. No matter how much you breathe through your mouth, there's no getting away from the foulness of it. My stomach rose in protest, but you can't retch in front of the patient. I just made it outside before I vomited a bitter stream onto the grass. My mouth was dry and sour and I wished I hadn't been so hasty to part with my water.

'Here. Have a swig.'

I straightened up and took a grateful pull at the flask that was offered. It wasn't what I expected.

'Whisky?'

The bloke it belonged to laughed. He was tall and broad-shouldered. Australian. Stronger built than most of our lads. Better fed. His arm was in a sling.

'There's more booze than water on this island just now. The ration I got this morning wouldn't bath a canary.'

'This is the British hospital. You lost?'

'I'm looking for someone,' he said. 'A Turkish prisoner called Tuzman. I've been to every hospital on the island and you're my last stop. Is he here?'

An enemy soldier. There's them who say don't treat him but Matron Morgan says we don't have enemies, we have patients. I like her for it. Morgan the Gorgon, we call her, but she's not all bad.

'He's in the small tent at the back of the marquee.'

'Can I see him?'

'Why?'

'I was detailed to guard him. The trench was hit by a shell and we were the only two left alive. I couldn't just leave him there. I got him down the gully to the beach and we bled into the sand together till the stretcher-bearers arrived.'

'You'll have to ask Matron. Her tent's over there.'

'Righto. Thanks.'

'I'm needed on the ward.'

He tipped his hat at me.

'Nice to meet you.'

'Aye. Thanks for the drink.'

As I walked away he called after me.

'Fancy a proper drink after your shift?'

A lot of the lads try it on. I don't blame 'em—we're all a long way from home. But this one wasn't wasting any time.

'I'm on all night.'

'Till?'

'Six.'

'I'll wait. We can go for a walk. Lemnos is lovely at dawn.'

I kept walking. He had to shout to cover the distance.

'Mike Warren. Australian Second Division. Walking wounded.'

'Nora Barnes. Voluntary Aid Detachment. Working.'

I ducked under the netting and went into the tent.

The ward was stifling. Three in the morning and the tent was still heavy with heat. It was unusually quiet. Some of the lads were managing to sleep, others were too far gone to make a sound. I could hear the sea breaking on the shingle beyond the rocks. I shut my eyes for a second and imagined wading into it and floating, spread-eagled in the waves. It was sweet torture.

'Nurse?' The whisper came from a bed at the end of the row. Archie Clarke was hauling himself up on his pillows, peering into the shadows across the tent. 'Nurse, where's Bert? Why is his bed empty?'

I heard the dread in his voice.

'It's alright Archie. Corporal Webb is in surgery.'

'I thought—'

'I know. Lie back now. You'll tear your stitches.'

Bert was older. The lads said he'd taken young Archie under his wing, looked after him. They were together in a trench when pieces of the same shell ripped into both their bodies. But Archie was lucky, his wounds had stayed healthy and he was healing.

'What are they doing to him?' he asked.

I plumped his pillows then pulled a chair up to the side of his bed.

'Amputation. He'll die if they don't.'

Archie closed his eyes. He went into himself for a minute.

'Lucky bastard.'

'He's lost a leg.'

'He's going home to his wife and kids. The war's over for him. I'd give a leg for that.'

He cried without making a sound. I held his hand and thought of all the times he must have kept his tears secret in the dark.

'Are you busy, Barnes?'

Matron Morgan stopped me on my way to the supply tent.

'We're out of dressings, Matron.'

'I'll see to that. I want you to keep Nurse Paget company.' She saw the look on my face. 'Is there a problem?'

'I'm not her favourite person.'

'Try to behave like an adult, Nurse Barnes. She's had bad news from home.'

'Sorry, Matron.'

'I left her in my tent.'

When I got there, Paget was sitting, reading a letter. I could see she'd been crying and she didn't look pleased to see me.

'Still mad at me?'

'No.'

'Just don't like me then?'

'I don't understand you.' She stood up and looked at me steadily. 'You think you know me but you don't. I came here to do a job and I'm going to do it with or without your good opinion.'

She headed past me to leave but I blocked her way.

'If it makes you feel better to have a go at me, carry on. I climb to the top of the hill myself and scream into the wind. You have to let off steam or you crack wide open.'

She looked suspicious. Fair enough. Why would she trust me?

'What do you want?'

'Matron sent me to check on you. She said you've had bad news.'

'You can tell Matron I'm fine.'

'But you aren't, are you?'

Her eyes filled with tears. She hesitated for a minute then sat back down. I couldn't bring myself to sit on Matron's starched bed so I perched on the end of the table. She was turning the letter over and over in her hands. It took her a while to start speaking.

'My brother James wrote to me,' she said at last. 'His schoolfriend was killed last week in France. Matthew.'

'I'm sorry.'

'He was in a trench, joking with another chap, and in the middle of a sentence he straightened up—laughing, they said—and a sniper shot him through the head.' She'd been calm so far but suddenly she crumpled. 'Why didn't he keep low? He knew he should keep low.'

'It was fast, at least.' Small comfort but better than none.

I stood up and opened the tent flap. The sunlight streamed in and lit her like a spotlight. She was smaller than me, plump and pretty, even with red eyes and a tear-stained face. I could see her in a lace dress, pouring tea in a fancy drawing room. She was wrong here, out of place.

'Go for a walk,' I told her. 'Get some air.'

She turned back before she left. The letter was still in her hand.

'They were friends all the way through school,' she said. 'Five of them, they were inseparable. And now there's just James. How long before it's his turn?'

I didn't speak. I don't think she expected an answer. We both knew it anyway.

*

He looked about thirty. Very thin, black hair, skin as grey as putty with a sheen of sweat from the infection that was killing

54

him. I bathed his face with a cold cloth and his eyes fluttered open, amber eyes, dull with fever. He shrank back when he saw me.

'It's alright. Easy now.'

His face was full of suspicion.

'I am Turkish,' he said. 'I am the enemy.'

He'd been delirious for days but suddenly he was back in the world, clear and present. It happens sometimes, at the end.

'You going to shoot me?' I asked.

'No.'

'Right then.'

His lips were dry and crusted. I held the cloth to them, feeling the heat coming off him.

'Where did you learn English?'

'I was a teacher before—' he closed his eyes, dark lashes against pale skin. His breathing was ragged. 'We are told it is a Holy War. That the Prophet says we must kill the infidel. But it is not Allah who sends us to Gallipoli, it is Man.'

'You should rest now.'

'What is your name?'

'Nurse Barnes.'

'I am Asil Tuzman.'

'Asil?'

'It means noble. I have not lived up to my name.'

'Why do you say that?'

'I have killed others to save myself.'

'That's war.'

He reached for my hand.

'Don't leave me.'

'I won't.'

'So much unfinished.' I could barely hear him. 'Are you still holding my hand?'

'Yes.'

'Don't leave me'.

'I'm here.'

'Don't leave me.'

I stayed till he didn't need anyone anymore.

*

There's a split seam up high in a corner of the marquee. You can see a small patch of sky, a few bright stars or, once in a while, the moon behind a cloud. Or watery pink streaks as another dawn breaks. I spent the last half hour of my shift watching the light change through the gap, sitting at Archie Clarke's bed again. I told him that Bert died on the operating table. He wasn't going home after all.

'At least he's out of it,' was all Archie said.

Outside the air was thick and heavy and the sky was darkening over the bay. There was nasty weather coming. The storms here are sudden and violent. I've never known wind like it and the rain streams down the hills and waterlogs everything, even with tarpaulins everywhere. But on the bright side, the sand flies and scorpions make themselves scarce till the sun comes out again.

'G'day.'

He was waiting where I'd left him, wearing the same cheeky grin.

'Are all Australians like you?'

'No. Some of them are really pushy!'

We walked down to the harbour and sat on a rock looking out to sea. Sixty miles away the guns of Gallipoli were making more patients for our beds and more bodies to be buried far from home. When the wind was in the right direction you could hear them booming across the water. Not today though. Everything was quiet and still while the storm gathered strength in the distance.

'So what did you do before the war, Nurse Barnes?'

'Worked in a cotton mill.'

'And when you weren't at work?'

'I chucked bricks through windows.'

'What?'

'Disrupted meetings. Chained myself to railings.'

I watched it dawn on him. 'You're one of those Suffragettes?'

'That's right.' I could see he didn't quite know what to make of it. The usual reaction. 'What about you?' I asked him. 'Before the war?'

'I'm a gardener,' he said. 'I like to watch things grow.'

'You'd get on with my dad—he lives for his allotment. There's not a lot of gardens where we live so he walks two miles every weekend to worship his veg.'

He laughed.

'You're a little bit barmy, aren't you, Nurse Barnes?'

He put his good arm around me and I didn't stop him.

'Tuzman,' I said. 'The Turkish prisoner. He died.'

He didn't say anything. Just nodded and looked out at the water. Back up the hill a band was playing 'Pack up your Troubles'. Some of the lads were singing along and their voices drifted down faintly to where we were sitting.

Pack up your troubles in your old kit bag
And smile, smile, smile.

Cheerful songs are the worst somehow.

'Why did you join up?' I asked him.

'The politicians said it was the war to end all wars—who wouldn't fight for that? They made it sound like a crusade.'

The music was getting louder. A unit of men came round the corner, marching down to the harbour to board ship. They were on their way back to the fighting. The column marched past us and one of the men blew me a kiss. He was stocky and small, almost dwarfed by his kit. The scar on his jaw was puckered and livid. It distorted the smile he gave me before they all marched out of sight.

What's the use of worrying?
It never was worthwhile.

I wanted to run after them, tell them not to go, tell them to desert, mutiny, anything—tell them to refuse to die. Thunder rumbled through the purple clouds over the sea. Mike leaned in and kissed me. Why not? We could all be dead tomorrow.

*

The storm lasted two days. The wind battered the tents non-stop, canvas flapping and straining against the creaking ropes. We took turns at going out into the downpour to hammer the pegs deeper, but the ground was a muddy swamp that couldn't hold them for long and every minute we expected the whole bloody lot to collapse on the patients. The only consolation was that the ships couldn't get through the weather so we had no new wounded.

Of course, that meant no sooner had the wind dropped and they could reach us than they all arrived at once and it was mayhem. Hundreds of dead and dying men crammed onto every deck. You could hear the screaming and moaning long before they docked. The stretcher-bearers were slipping and sliding in mud on their way up the hill and some of the walking wounded went down and just stayed where they fell till we helped them back to their feet.

I was buckling under the weight of a big bloke with a shattered leg when Paget ran out of the laundry tent with her arms full of sheets.

'We're out of bandages,' she said as I lowered him onto a tarpaulin. 'Matron sent me to tear these into strips.'

'Give some here.'

We ducked under an awning to keep the sheets out of the rain. We were both soaked to the skin and covered in mud and blood. Paget kept breaking off tearing the sheets to scratch her head through her sodden cap.

'Visitors?' I asked.

'I think so.'

'Still got all your hair under there?'

'Yes.'

'It needs to go.'

'Cut it off?'

'Saves on kerosene shampoo. You keep tearing. I'll take these in.'

I only got as far as the entrance to the ward where Matron grabbed them off me.

'Water's running out,' she said. 'Go to the kitchen tents and tell them to start boiling rainwater. Lots of it!'

I did as I was told. No shortage of rain at least. I was on my way to help Paget again when a little chubby corporal staggered towards me, part-carrying, part-dragging a much taller bloke on his back.

'Help him,' he pleaded as I ran towards them. 'It's my brother. Please help.'

His legs gave way as I reached him and they both dropped to the ground, the Corporal gasping for breath. One look at the other was enough to know that he'd done all the breathing he was ever going to do. His brother had hauled a dead weight

58

through the rain and mud to my feet.

I knelt down and helped the little bloke sit up, leaning him against a rock. He had a bloody bandage around his head, over one ear. He smelt musty and sour, of stale sweat and wet cloth. There were flecks of grey in his hair and in the stubble on his hamster cheeks.

'What's your name?' I asked him.

'Corporal Dobson,' he said. 'George Dobson.'

I took hold of his hand. 'I'm sorry, George. Your brother's gone.'

'Eddie.'

'Eddie's dead. I'm sorry.'

He didn't move. He didn't look across to his brother's body, sprawled where he had dropped him. He looked at me with uncomprehending eyes.

'He can't be dead,' he said. 'He's younger than me.'

When I finally got back to the tent, Paget was standing with a pair of scissors in her hand, her hair loose over her shoulders and down her back. Beautiful gold waves, long and heavy. She turned to me as I came in, her face flushed, a mixture of shame and sorrow in her eyes.

'I can't do it,' she said. 'I can't cut it.'

I nodded. I remembered chopping mine and it was harder than I expected. All the men out there being blown to pieces and we were grieving for our hair.

'It needs doing though.'

'I know.'

She held out the scissors, with a sad little smile, and I took hold of them. Her hair was alive with lice. I wrapped it around my hand in thick sections and cut it off close to her scalp, dropping the lengths onto a newspaper at our feet. She stood very still but I could feel her trembling as the pile of hair on the floor grew higher and she felt the new sensation of air on her head and neck. When I was finished, I put my hands on her shoulders and she leant back against me briefly, without a word. For a moment the war seemed a world away. Then she moved.

'I'll take it to the incinerator.'

'I'll do it.' I bent and wrapped the newspaper into a bundle. 'You need to wash your head with kerosene shampoo, to kill the eggs. There's some in the supply tent.'

'Thank you, Nora,' she said as she left.

I didn't realise I was holding my breath till she was gone.

Later, we hung our soaking uniforms to steam next to the stove and I made cocoa. Rose was sitting on her bed in her petticoat. She kept putting a hand to her shorn head, as if she couldn't believe it was hers. She looked young and vulnerable.

'It'll grow again,' I said.

'Yes.'

'You'll be more comfortable now.'

'Thank you. You've been very kind.'

'That's alright.'

'Could we make a fresh start, do you think?'

She smiled. A bit wan, but it was a brave effort, considering. She was a long way from her pampered life and I'd have put money on her running back to it before now, but she was still here.

'We got off on the wrong foot,' I said. 'It happens to me a lot.'

'You have strong views.'

'You can always tell me to shut up.'

'And would you?'

'Probably not.'

The shift had lasted eighteen hours but the boats were finally empty. The wards were crowded and the mortuary tents so full we had to lay rows of bodies outside in the rain. Don't suppose it can hurt them now. Emergencies aside, we had eight hours off. Some of the girls were living it up in the YMCA tent but I just wanted some sleep. I finished my cocoa and thankfully crawled into bed. The creaky springs and lumpy mattress felt like a pile of feather eiderdowns. I lay there for a while, conscious of Rose settling down a few feet away, but exhaustion won out and I started to drift off. Then her voice brought me back to wakefulness with a jolt.

'Why are you here? If you disapprove of this war so heartily, why did you come?'

I didn't answer.

'Nora? Are you asleep?'

'No.' I said at last.

'Are you a Pacifist?'

That made me laugh.

'No. I'm not. I'm really not.'

'So isn't it right to stand up to your enemies?'

I sat up. She was up too, sitting on the edge of her bed. Her face was open, puzzled. I felt sorry for her. She didn't have a clue how the world worked. Only the establishment version she'd been fed her whole life. I didn't know where to start.

'The thing is,' I said, 'you and me see different people as enemies.'

'I don't understand.'

Course she didn't. But I launched in anyway.

'The King, the Tsar and the Kaiser, they're all one to me. I've got more in common with the workers in Germany than I have with our government. They've done me more harm than any foreigner ever has.'

'How?'

'By keeping me in my place. By looking after the rich at the expense of the poor.'

She looked shocked, almost bewildered.

'Are you a Socialist?'

'If it's good enough for Keir Hardie, it's good enough for me.'

'I heard him speak once. Against the war. He was jeered off the platform.'

'When he spoke in Parliament he was drowned out by MPs singing the national anthem—Labour MPs from his own benches behind him. But he'll be proved right soon enough.'

She flushed pink with indignation.

'The Germans invaded Belgium—'

'And the British Empire invaded half the world.'

I considered just stopping right there, honestly, I did. I know from long experience that waking somebody up to a different view of the world is a slow business. It takes patience and tolerance and, granted, I don't have much of either, but I wanted to do right by Rose Paget. Much better to stop for now and go to sleep. Tomorrow is another day. But she pressed on and so did I and it all went downhill from there.

'We're fighting to preserve our way of life.'

'Well I can see why you'd want to preserve yours.'

'What does that mean?'

'Private education, parlourmaids and picnics on the river, was it? I had poor schooling, never enough food on the table and twelve-hour days in the mill. Why would anyone fight to preserve that?'

'It isn't about the class system.'

'Everything is about the class system.' We were glaring at each other across the tent. 'Look,' I said, 'you've been told we're defending ourselves against an evil enemy and you swallowed it. Don't you think the Germans were told the same thing? It's what governments always do when they want people to fight and die for them. It's the easiest lie in the world.'

'Then why are we at war?'

'Power and profit. What all wars are fought for.'

She looked at me with utter contempt. Her eyes were bright with anger in a pale face.

'All those men being slaughtered, making the ultimate sacrifice for an ideal, for something bigger than themselves and you reduce it to a sordid, cynical ploy. Shame on you.'

'I'm not ashamed. I'm angry.' I pushed my blankets aside and got up. 'I don't deny the heroism. What sickens me is the entitled feeding on it for their own benefit.'

I grabbed my uniform. It was still damp but I threw it on.

'What are you doing?'

'Going out. Going up the hill to have a shout.'

'About me?'

'You and everyone like you. You've got a brain, use it. You're being manipulated by a system that doesn't even give you the right to vote against it. Open your eyes!'

I pulled my cape on and stormed out into the rain. So much for a fresh start, eh? Well done me.

*

'It's nearly midnight,' Mike said.

'So?'

'August 4th tomorrow.'

'Oh.' I hadn't realised.

The storm had passed over and it was a beautiful, calm night. The green lights and red crosses on the hospital ships reflected fairground colours in the harbour as we sat listening to the waves.

'Drink?'

He held out the flask that he'd offered the first time we met. I took it and held it up.

'A toast. To Tom, Jack and Bill.'

'Who are they?'

'The Taylor brothers. We grew up on the same street. They enlisted together, trained together and died together at Mons.'

Mike took the flask back.

'To my Uncle Fred and my mate Barney.' He took a swig. 'And to all the other poor buggers who'll never go home.'

There was a burst of laughter from the YMCA tent along the beach and I suddenly felt the need for company.

'Cup of tea?' I asked and Mike nodded.

Inside, the tent was crowded and hot. It smelt of warm earth and stale air. An old gramophone was playing and two of the girls were trying to teach a couple of blokes from the catering corps how to waltz. We gave it a wide berth and sat at a table near the counter. Mike collected two teas and added a nip from his flask when the chaplain wasn't looking.

'Isn't that your roomie?'

I looked up to see Rose coming in and my heart quickened. We'd been on separate shifts since the night of the row and had barely seen each other. I hadn't told Mike anything about it, so he waved her over before I could stop him. She looked across at me, uncertainly. She seemed worn out, battered. I pulled out a chair.

'Sit down. Have a cuppa.'

She sank down, took the cup and drank.

'This isn't tea.'

'Added ingredient,' Mike leaned over and offered to top her up.

'Why not?' she said. 'A year. A year today.'

'A whole year.' Mike said. 'I was planting a honeysuckle when I heard. Probably all over the hedge by now.'

'I was at an open-air meeting on Kersal Moor. They announced it from the platform.'

'I was buying a hat,' said Rose. 'I was pretending life was going on just as it always had and buying a white hat with pink roses on it.'

She held out her cup for another tot and Mike obliged.

'Plenty more where that came from,' he grinned. 'I know a bloke.'

The dancers had given up, the gramophone had stopped and one of the girls was banging out a tune on the old piano in the corner. The crowd round her were singing along. 'I don't want to join the army.' I had to shout so Mike could hear me.

'My great gran was transported to Australia.'

'What for?'

'Breaking looms. I'm descended from a convict.'

'Aren't we all?'

'You too?'

He nodded.

'My mum's grampa stole a walking stick from a doctor in Dublin and ended up on a chain gang.'

The singing was getting louder.

I don't want a bayonet up me arsehole,
I don't want me bollocks shot away.
I'd rather stay in England,
In Merry, Merry England
And fornicate me bleedin' life away!

I looked across at Rose to see her reaction but she didn't seem to notice. Her eyes were bright in a flushed face. Too much of Mike's special tea.

'What about you, Rose?' Mike asked, laughing. 'Any desperate criminals in your family?'

'The Pagets? Of course not. Solid citizens, every one.' Her voice was brittle. 'Pillars of the community. God, King and Country. Everything Nurse Barnes despises.'

Mike turned questioning eyes in my direction and I shrugged.

'We don't agree on much, me and Nurse Paget.'

Rose's colour deepened. She waved her cup at me and what was left in it showered onto the table.

'She thinks I'm a naive fool.'

Mike was mopping up the spill, taking the cup from her hand and giving us both placating looks at the same time. Not bad for a bloke with one arm in a sling. Me and Rose were eye to eye across the dripping table. I had a thousand things to say and I'm sure she had too. But the girl on the piano started a solo in a sweet soprano voice and the room hushed around her and held its communal breath as she sang, 'There's No Place Like Home'.

Home. Home. Sweet, Sweet Home.

Every face softened. I felt my anger fade and die. The song finished and in the sudden, sacred quiet, I looked at Rose and she was crying. I reached out and touched the tips of her fingers. They were cold. She looked up at me, the tears drying on her face, and then she looked away.

'I never wore that hat,' she said.

She was still awake when I got back to the tent. She sat up as I came in and lit a candle. I sat on my bed, too tired to get undressed, and there was an awkward silence.

'You never answered my question,' she said at last. 'Why are you here?'

'You're like a dog at a bone aren't you?'

'I want to understand.'

I couldn't argue with that. But it wasn't easy. I tried to find the right words.

'Truth is, it was a mistake and it's taken till now to admit it to myself. But Mrs Pankhurst suspended the Union for the duration and said we should support the war effort. She's no Socialist, I know, and her and Christabel have shown their true colours since war broke out, but I felt I had to do something, to be useful. I was wrong. My comrades at home all joined the peace movement and that's what I should have done. My mate Daisy was mad as hell at me for coming. She said I'm condoning the war by being here—and she's right.'

'You're helping the men.'

'Peace would help them more.'

I worked up the energy to take my uniform off and get between the covers. Rose turned on her side, facing me across the gap between our beds. The candle didn't give much light but I could see the questions in her eyes.

'I came here because I thought we were fighting for a better world.'

'Well there's no greater cause than that.'

'But will it be better?'

'It'll be emptier.'

'Hearts at peace, Brooke says. How will anyone ever know peace again after this? I'd like to go to Skyros one day, stand by his grave in that olive grove and tell him how lucky he was to die with his ideals intact.'

'Does that mean yours aren't?'

She turned on her back and I could see her profile as she stared up at the canvas above us.

'Before my training, I'd never seen a man's body.' Her voice was almost a whisper. 'The first time I did, it was a dead boy—eighteen at the most. He was beautiful. Except for the bloody hole where the back of his skull should have been. I remember thinking this shouldn't be my first memory of a man naked. But it is. It always will be.'

'I'm sorry.'

'It isn't worth it. Whether I'm right about the war or you are, it isn't worth it.'

Life has a way of surprising you, doesn't it? We come from different worlds. Our paths should never have crossed. Yet there we were baring our souls, in a small tent, on an island hundreds of miles from home. She turned over and pulled the covers around her. All I could see was the top of her cropped head against the pillow. Her voice was muffled.

'Do you believe in God, Nora?'

'No.'

'In Heaven?'

'No.'

'Isn't that bleak?'

'Depends how you look at it. If you only have one life, you'd better make it count.'

'And then we're just dust?'

She wanted some comfort.

'What does it say in your Brooke poem—a richer dust?'

There shall be, in that rich earth, a richer dust concealed.

'Well, if we've lived well, loved well and done our best to leave the world a bit better than we found it, that's what we'll be. Richer.'

It was the best I could do.

*

There's been an outbreak of dysentery in the trenches. We always have some on every boat, exhausted and dehydrated, but today, all but three of the new intake were burning with fever and covered in shit and vomit. Cleaning them up was the first job. Stripping off the uniforms and burning the worst to avoid infection as best we can. We'll be lucky if half the medical staff don't come down with it anyway. There isn't enough water for showers or baths so, if they were fit enough, we washed them down in the sea, wrapped them in a blanket and put them on tarpaulins away from the wards. When and if new uniforms arrive is anybody's guess.

It's the flies, one of them told me. They're everywhere. Clouds of fat, black flies droning around their faces, lining the walls of the trenches, feeding on the corpses and the latrines and then swarming onto the food in a sluggish, bloated mass.

Suddenly I couldn't breathe. I was sucking in air, chest heaving, heart thumping, dizzy and shaking.

'You alright, Nurse?' a passing stretcher-bearer turned and stopped.

I couldn't answer him. I could hear the blood pounding in my head and I was sinking. All I knew was his grip on my arm. He had pale, freckled hands with long fingers and a few golden hairs catching the sunlight. His jacket sleeve was fraying at the wrist.

'Easy now,' he said. 'It's alright.'

Next thing I knew I was leaning against a tree trunk behind the marquee, sitting on the dry, dusty ground, and he was holding a cup of water to my lips.

'I've never fainted in my life,' I said sheepishly. I was more embarrassed than anything else. 'I don't know what happened.'

He stood up and looked down at me. Under the dirt and sweat, his face was as freckled as his hands. His eyes were weary.

'You'll be fine now. Sit for a while.'

'I'm on duty.'

'Give yourself a minute. Drink that water. I have to go.'

He turned and moved away.

'Thanks,' I called after him. He raised a hand and walked round the tent and out of sight.

I closed my eyes for a minute and leant back against the tree. It was shady and cool and there was a faint, sweet smell of wild thyme drifting down from the hills. I'd walked up there with

Mike on his last night here. We'd stood among the purple flowers and looked down at the hospital and the wide sea. The ship that would take him away was moored ready in the harbour. His sling was gone and he held me in both arms, pulled me to him, so I could hear his heart beating next to mine.

I looked up into his face. Blue eyes with black lashes. Put in with a smutty finger my gran would have said if she'd seen them. It's the Irish in him, from his Dublin convict. He smiled down at me.

'You should come to Oz, after the war. You'll love it.'

After the war. I couldn't even imagine it. But it was our last night so I played the game.

'We could find where my great gran is buried. Pay our respects.'

I wanted to tell him that I knew he was scared, that he didn't need to pretend. Instead, we made plans for the future, looking out across the miles of sea that would ebb and flow between us from now on. The sun went down, the sky darkened and he held out his hand.

'Let's have a dance.'

'There's no music.'

'So?'

We danced close under the moon for a long time. When he started to unbutton my uniform I took hold of his hand.

'This isn't love,' I said. 'You know that?'

'I know.'

'I'm no virgin.'

'Neither am I.'

I let go of his fingers, let them do their work. All we have is moments.

*

'My brother has been awarded the DSO,' said Rose.

We were in the supply tent, counting the last of the sheets and blankets.

'Captain James Paget, for conspicuous gallantry in action.'

Matron had sent us to do an inventory. A new offensive had doubled the hospital boats in the last day or two and it was nearly empty.

'You must be proud.'

'A few months ago I would have been bursting with pride. Now I don't know how I feel.'

'I make that two dozen sheets and eight blankets.'

'He ran into this war, Nora. Why do you think it was it so easy for the government to win our consent?'

I'd opened the floodgates with Rose, right enough. She was full of questions. Whenever we were together, at some point she'd start asking for my two-penneth on something. I could see her weighing it up and making connections.

'It's always easy. People want to believe in something and the press sell them a story. If it wasn't for the papers, the war would-n't have lasted a month.'

'But why would the newspapers lie?'

'Look who owns them. The establishment takes care of its own. Four blankets. That's a dozen.'

She leaned, half sitting, on a wide, empty shelf. Her cheeks were flushed with the heat and there was a light beading of sweat on her brow and lip. She pulled off her cap and dabbed at her face. Her hair was growing in again, curling gold around her ears and she ran her hands through it.

'You never look hot,' she said indignantly.

'Course I do.'

'No, you're cool as a cucumber. Tall and pale whilst I'm short and pink, blowing steam like a kettle.'

'Of the two of us, I think I'm the one full of hot air.'

She laughed.

'It's all the thinking. My head is in a whirl.'

'I noticed.'

She whacked me with her cap before cramming it back on her head.

'It's alright for you. You've been a rebel all your life, but I've never questioned till now. I didn't even know there was anything to ask.'

'Question everything. That's how I was raised.' I looked behind us. 'See there. Three more sheets. Pass them over.'

'You said your education was poor.' She fetched them and added them to the pile.

'It was short. I was in the mill at twelve.'

'But you know so much. My education cost a small fortune

and I know nothing! They taught me how to play the piano, embroider and speak a little French.'

'It was passed on to me. I come from a long line of fighting women.'

'Your great grandmother? The one who died in Australia?'

'Hannah. Her daughter Clara marched with the Chartists and her granddaughter Grace was sacked from three mills for trying to organise a trade union.'

'Grace is your mother?'

'Aye.'

'And now there's you.'

'Now there's me.'

'It's like a chain. Hannah to Clara, Clara to Grace, Grace to you, you to me.'

'And you to whoever you like. That's how it works.'

'Don't you ever lose heart?'

'Ten times a day.'

'Then what?'

'Then you carry on. My gran used to say, you just put one foot in front of the other. That's all you can do.' I got to my feet. 'Twenty-seven sheets and twelve blankets. Come on. We'd better report back.'

*

Winter came quickly to Lemnos. The last thing on my mind, when I imagined a Greek island, was snow, but for days now, we've had a world of white. The trees on the hills, the rocks at the shore and the boats in the harbour all sparkling in the watery sunlight. And that unnatural quiet that snow brings, a deadening of sound and a strange stillness.

It's been snowing at Gallipoli too. Snow on the beaches. Beautiful snow, covering lots of things that aren't. The boats are full of frostbite cases, swollen black toes and fingers, lots of amputations. Every morning in the trenches they find men frozen to death, icicles hanging from them like white ribbons.

Rose had been on the night shift. When she came out of the marquee I was waiting for her, my heart thudding in my chest like shellfire.

'Have you got a minute? I've something to tell you.'

We walked down to the water. There were a few snowflakes still drifting in the sea breeze and they settled on us, white spots on our dark coats that melted as soon as they landed. Rose had her arms wrapped around her body. Her nose and cheeks were pinched with the cold.

'You're leaving, aren't you?' Her breath misted in front of her face.

'I have to.'

'I know.'

'No. It's not what you think. I'm going to have a baby.'

For a minute she was so still and her face so blank that I wondered if she'd heard what I said. Then she took a step and threw her arms around me. Right away, I felt comforted. For the first time since I realised I was pregnant, I didn't feel afraid.

She pulled away and looked up at me.

'Mike?'

I nodded.

'Does he know?'

'I've written to him. But I don't expect him to "do the right thing". I don't want that.'

'Don't you?'

'I've never wanted that.'

I searched her face for a sign that she understood what I meant, but I couldn't be sure what she was thinking. I was carrying Mike's baby. How could she possibly know what I wanted? At last, she broke the silence.

'What will you do?'

'Go home to Salford.'

'Your family—?'

'They'll get used to the idea.'

My eyes were fixed on hers. Suddenly I saw something in them that made hope explode in me like a firework.

'What?' I asked. 'What is it?'

'Does it have to be Salford?'

'No,' I said slowly. 'Why?'

'I inherited my grandmother's house—a big, old place in Ealing.' She took my mittened hands in hers. 'It's sitting empty and, I've been thinking, I could open a school. A free school. A progressive school for girls.'

'And?'

'And I've been thinking we could do it together.'

Her eyes were bright with excitement, big brown eyes searching my face for an answer and, when she saw it, they filled with happy tears.

'Yes?'

'Yes.'

'Really?'

'Yes, really.'

We stood smiling at each other like a pair of idiots until I pulled her into me and we stayed there, clasped together on the wintry shore for I don't know how long. I think I was in a kind of shock. I could hardly remember what I'd agreed to. Just that it was with Rose and that was enough.

At long last, we walked back up the slope, our footsteps crunching on the frozen grass. The tents and guy ropes were frosted white and glittering like tinsel. Inside was pain and fear and death. Outside, it looked like fairyland.

'I'll still be fighting for the vote,' I said.

'Of course.'

'And all the rest of it. The vote is just the beginning.'

'Yes. All the rest of it.'

We reached our tent and went in.

'I'll get some cocoa,' she said. 'You sit down and rest.'

In the dim light and the quiet, I began to settle. I watched her light the stove and gather the mugs. Slowly the questions started.

'A school?'

'Why not?'

'We don't know where to start.'

'I'll hire people who do.'

'A free school. How will you make it pay?'

'It doesn't need to.'

'Sorry?'

She turned to me with the saucepan in her hand. She was smiling, a bit sheepish.

'I inherited money as well as the house. There's a great deal of it.'

'A great deal?'

'A very great deal.'

'Oh. Right.'

She came to sit beside me.

'I'm sorry. I know you don't approve.'

'When did I say that? I approve of money, if it's spread around.'

Her face was earnest, determined.

'We can build something out of this wreckage. We can make a future for those girls. And for ourselves. I did nothing to earn my money, but I'll do something with it, I swear to you.'

I took the saucepan from her and put it on the floor. Then I took her face in my hands. We stared at each other for a long, still moment and then I kissed her. She tasted of salt and snow.

1926

A COUPLE of theatres have closed their doors because of the strike but most are still open. We had a full house tonight. Two thousand people cheering Fred and Adele Astaire is a sight for sore eyes, I can tell you. Alright, I'm at the back of the chorus, but I've made it to the West End at last and, with more Music Halls becoming Picture Palaces every week, I'm counting my blessings and saving my pennies for a rainy day.

'We've had the rainy days,' Humph says when he hears me.

He's right. We've had a bleedin' monsoon. But we're still here.

When I come out after the show, it doesn't look like London. Too empty. Too quiet. The theatre crowds are thinning out and the streets are nearly free of traffic. A few people have driven their cars into town, there are bikes and the odd pony and trap but nothing like usual, no trams, no buses. In the suburbs, volunteers are keeping public transport running; students with posh voices are sitting behind protective wire mesh, with a Copper next to them, to keep order. Fat fucking chance. Every bus I've seen has had a brick through half its windows. The toffs don't get it, they think the strike is just a game, a lark. Tell that to the betrayed miners and their starving kids, I say. Tell that to the pickets on the docks, facing soldiers with machine guns. When this is over, the students will go back to their Universities and Medical Schools and carry on with their comfortable lives, whilst the workers are hammered again, shat on from a great height, as always.

> It's the same the whole world over,
> It's the poor what gets the blame.
> It's the rich what gets the pleasure,
> Ain't it just a bloomin' shame.

Marie Lloyd sang that at the party she threw for her fiftieth at the old Bedford Music Hall and we all joined in the chorus, raising the rafters. We were laughing but we sang it with feeling cos most of us know the truth of it. That was the last time I saw her, though I stood with hundreds of others, watching her funeral car drive through Golders Green. Gone but not forgotten, Marie. The end of an era. The world she knew, the Halls I grew up in, they're becoming a thing of the past. The flickers are taking over, Buster Keaton and Douglas Fairbanks. That's life, ain't it? Things change.

I'm crossing Old Compton Street when a swanky silver Bentley glides to a stop at the kerb beside me and the window rolls down. Some fat cat trying his luck. My first thought is cheeky bastard but a little bit of me can't help thinking, 'still got it, girl'. I just keep walking. My digs are a few minutes away and I've got a nice pan of stew waiting on the stove.

'Daisy!'

I look back and there's a blonde head leaning out and a gloved hand waving. It's Milly. Or Lilly. Same old problem. She gets out of the car, all furs and fringes and bobbed hair and gives me a big hug. I look for the other one and she sees what I'm doing and shakes her head.

'Milly's in America. She's gone to Hollywood.'

'You must be missing her.'

'Something awful. But she's got a contract with King Vidor. You'll be seeing her in the pictures before long.'

'Why didn't you go with her?'

She smiles at me and takes off her glove. There's a massive diamond on her finger.

'Bleedin' hell! Who did you rob?'

'Two weeks from now I'll be Mrs Albert Crabbe.'

'Albert Crabbe, the Marmalade King?'

'That's the one.'

That explains the car. Lilly Winsome has landed on her feet.

'Congratulations.'

'I'm giving up the stage. I don't want to go solo and Albert wants to travel anyway. Suits me. I've never been further than Dover! We're going to see the world then find a nice house in the country and settle down.'

'Sounds lovely.'

'Liar! You'd curl up and die without the theatre and your politics, I know you.'

'You're right,' I laugh. 'But good luck to you, girl. I'm happy for you.'

A few drops of rain have been falling whilst we're talking and suddenly the heavens open and it's chucking it down. Lilly grabs my arm.

'Get in the car. I'll give you a lift home.'

'I'm just round the corner.'

'Don't matter. Come on.' As we run to the Bentley, a uniformed chauffeur gets out and opens the door for us. I give Lilly a look and she laughs. 'Get out of the rain, Tommy!' she calls to him as we pile inside.

'Less of the Tommy,' says the chauffeur from the front seat. 'You're supposed to call me Thompson, remember?'

'Bleedin' hell,' I say, looking at the plush leather and polished wood stretching out around me. 'I've had digs smaller than this!'

Lilly is shaking the rain from her furs and patting her smooth hair into place.

'Shut up, the pair of you.'

'You can take the girl out of Stepney,' I say, and we laugh.

'Mad ain't it? Albert's away on business and he's left me in a suite at The Langham, with the car and a wad of cash to play with. I still can't believe it.'

'Where to?' asks Tommy.

'St Anne's Court,' I tell him.

Lilly leans forward.

'Come back with me and have some supper. We can have a proper catch up.' She sees me hesitating. 'Please?'

'I don't want to take advantage.'

'Oh behave. Let me treat you. For old times' sake.'

I think about my tiny flat with an Italian family thumping and shouting on the floor above and an all-night Chinese restaurant below. I've never set foot in The Langham. No contest really.

'Alright then, I will,' I say. 'Thanks, Lilly.'

The stew can wait.

I lean back on the soft leather as the Bentley glides through the quiet streets like an ocean liner. It's really chucking it down now and, through the rain on the windows, I see a few walkers bent against the weather. On one corner, a group of men are huddled against the wall for shelter, caps pulled down, hands in the pockets of their thin coats. They watch the car pass by them in silence, their faces drawn and sullen. They look tense, on the edge of anger. I don't blame 'em. What this car cost would feed a working family for a year.

'Why aren't you in Camberwell with Humph?' Lilly asks out of nowhere.

'I don't live with him.'

'Why not? It's a nice little house.'

'I know.'

'And it's half yours, ain't it?'

'Not really. He put me on the deeds, so I had the property qualification for the vote.'

'Bless him.'

'I know.'

'Don't tell me he wouldn't like you there anyway. Why don't you take pity on the poor bloke and marry him?'

'We're alright as we are.'

'I remember taking you there after your first time in Holloway. A right state you were in. He put you in his bed and slept in the spare room like a proper gent, but we saw the way he looked at you. Has he never popped the question?' She laughs. 'He has! I can see it in your face.'

'Are we nearly there? I'm starving.'

'Tommy?'

'Two minutes. And it's Thompson.'

'Come on,' says Lilly. 'Cough it up.'

'He asked me. Before the war.'

'I knew it! Why didn't you say yes?'

'I was too busy.'

The movement took everything I had in those days. I was in and out of prison, hiding from the law. I didn't have the space for anything else.

'Well the war's over now. And we've got the vote.'

'Not all of us. I had to cheat to get it and most working women aren't so lucky.'

'There'll always be something with you, won't there?'

'I hope so.'

Her face lights up with a sudden memory.

'Do you remember the time the Coppers raided the safe house?' she laughs. 'And you climbed out of the window and ran across the rooftops to get away?'

'I remember it was raining and the tiles were slippy as an ice rink! I nearly broke my neck more than once before I found a drainpipe to shin down.'

'You're a nutter, Daisy Daniels.'

'Thanks for that.'

The car stops and right away the door is opened from outside. It isn't Tommy this time, it's a hotel doorman who gives a little bow as we get out and climb the steps to the front entrance. He's wearing a very fancy coat and hat. He's better dressed than me. I admit I feel a bit tatty in my everyday clobber, but I straighten my back and walk into the foyer like I own the place. I've as much right to be here as anyone else.

I swear I've never seen as much gilt and marble in my entire life. There's more than the fanciest theatre foyer I've ever seen. It's another bleedin' world. Through an archway across from the reception desk, there's a massive room with chandeliers and plush chairs arranged round little tables. Drinks on all of 'em and lots of silver champagne buckets draped with white linen napkins. A group of people in evening dress are standing around a wireless on the end of the bar, listening to the news. Waiting to hear if the revolution has kicked off yet, I expect. Worrying we'll go the way of Russia. They haven't got a clue. This strike was over before it started. Them in charge are making sure of that.

I can't hear the newsreader but I can guess what he's saying. Doing what the BBC do, pretending to be neutral but dancing to the government's tune. The British Falsehood Corporation, the miners call it. Yesterday they reported that four hundred men had gone back to work at Gallis Green Colliery. Most people would swallow that, think the strike was breaking down. How would they know that Gallis Green has been closed for years? Thing is, everyone knows what the miners suffer, there's a lot of sympathy for 'em and the government can't have that, so they set the propaganda machine in motion. They did it to the Suffragettes, they did it in the war and they're doing it now. And it works. Every time. That's the pisser.

Lilly collects her key from a superior type behind the desk who looks me up and down as he hands it over. Alright, I'm not dressed to impress but he's wearing a stupid uniform for fuck's sake. No snob like a working-class snob. I give him a big cheeky smile and a wink before I follow Lilly to the lift.

'I've ordered supper in the room, so we can be nice and cosy,' she says as we glide upwards.

There's another liveried bloke in with us, just in case we don't know how to press a button. He stands like a ramrod, not looking at either of us. Orders I suppose. Knowing his place. We step out on the top floor, Lilly throws open the doors to the suite and it's the most beautiful set of rooms I've ever seen. Thick carpets and glossy furniture, fancy little lamps dotted around and flower arrangements in huge vases. She's standing in the middle of it all, beaming at me.

'What a set up, eh?'

We've hardly got our coats off when there's a tap at the door and two waiters wheel in a trolley piled with silver domes. They set it all out on the table. Wine in an ice bucket, delicate china, heavy linen napkins, it's all perfect.

'Pile in,' she tells me, and I help myself to chicken and salmon, warm bread rolls and cold white wine. It's heaven.

Through the windows, London spreads out for miles in every direction, thousands of lights on thousands of streets, as far as you can see. From the top floor, it all seems a long way off, safe and protected from the worst. No wonder rich people can hold themselves aloof from politics, feel it's beneath them. The world can't hurt them like it can the poor. This is Lilly's life now. Silver dishes and fresh flowers. Clean and warm and easy. I don't begrudge her reaching for it.

She refills my glass, we kick our shoes off and curl up in plush armchairs, open a second bottle. I'm feeling nicely warm and fuzzy-headed.

'Thanks for this Lilly,' I say. 'It's a real treat.'

Her dress is made of something shimmery that catches the light when she moves. Still a stunner. No wonder the Marmalade King was bowled over. As if she can read my thoughts, she sits forward.

'I'm not in love with him. Albert. He knows that. But I'm fond of him and we get on. We'll be happy enough. I don't ask for more since I lost Bill.'

I get it. She's one of thousands whose dreams of happiness are buried in the Flanders mud. Her Bill died on the first day of the Somme. Humph was luckier. The mustard gas took a lung and he left the cheeky smile I loved out there in hell, but he came back when so many didn't.

'I wish you all the best,' I say, and I mean it.

Companionship and a bit of luxury. There's worse lives.

'Did he never ask again?'

'What?'

'Humph. Was it just the once?'

'It was a long time ago.'

'It's like getting blood out of a stone!' She gives me a grin. 'Come on, spill the beans.'

'Why are you so interested in Humphrey Carter all of a sudden?'

'Cos Milly and me always thought you two were made for each other. And we're not getting any younger, are we?'

'Alright, alright. Keep your hair on.' I hold out my glass and she obliges. 'We fell out when he enlisted, if you must know. There I was campaigning day and night for peace and he marches off to war. I was livid! I tore him off a right strip. Then I spent four years fretting that he'd be killed and the last thing I said to him was fuck off!'

'Gawd almighty, girl! Do you love him, or don't you?'

'Oh, I love him.'

'Right then. So?'

I think about saying nothing but, in for a penny, I suppose. So I tell her.

'It was hard when he came back. I know I've no right to complain when he's alive and so many aren't—'

'Don't be daft.'

'He still has bad dreams. He wakes up screaming.'

I just hold him till he stops shaking. I try to imagine what it was like for them out there, but it's not real to me, the horror, like it is to him.

'I'm sorry, Daisy. I never thought.'

'It's alright. We have some good times. We take each day as it comes.'

Lilly pours out the last of the wine.

'Shall I order another?'

'Not for me, girl. I'm nodding off.'

'Me too. There's a spare room here, if you want it. Then Tommy can take you home in the morning.'

'You sure?'

'Course.'

'Alright then.'

She lends me a nightie, all silk and lace. The bed is big and soft with crisp sheets and an embroidered cover. I snuggle down and smile up at her.

'I could get used to this!'

'How the other half live.'

'That's right.'

She looks solemn suddenly, a bit embarrassed.

'I won't let it go to my head,' she says. 'I won't forget where I came from.'

'I know you won't.'

'Albert has no airs and graces. He's a self-made man. He's always saying he knows how lucky he is.'

'Even luckier to have you.'

'Behave!'

'I mean it. I'm happy you and Milly are both living the dream. You deserve it.'

'Thanks, Daisy.'

'Is she coming back for the wedding?'

'We're going over there. Married in Hollywood—fancy that!'

The warm bed is getting to me and I'm drifting off.

'Give my love to Rudolph Valentino.'

'Get in the queue!'

'Story of my life.'

She leans in and kisses my cheek. 'Night, girl. Sweet dreams.'

'Night, Lilly.'

I'm asleep before she closes the door.

*

'Not a Penny off the Pay! Not a Minute on the Day!'

I can hear the chanting from streets away and when I turn into Trafalgar Square, the noise gets deafening. There's hundreds of people with placards and red flags waving in the breeze. Somebody's fastened a massive banner to the bottom of Nelson's Column—Workers of the World, Unite! A deputation of miners from all over the country is standing on the steps of the National Gallery and Mr Cook, their leader, is giving a speech through a loud hailer.

I push through the crowd to get a better look at him. If you believed the press and the government, A J Cook is the devil incarnate. One day, he's incompetent, the next he's a danger to our peace and security. Now, I ask you, how can he be both? Truth is, he's neither. He's a danger to them in power, is what he is, and the miners love him for it.

'Everything the workers have,' he's saying,' has been fought for, with blood, sweat and tears. It has been wrested from the hands of power against all odds. And still it is precious little, still we work and starve to increase the wealth and comfort of those who oppress us. Now, they want us to do more, to work longer for less. They tell us we must suffer to put the country back on its feet. But do they suffer? No, they do not. Do they work for less? Never. Landowners like the Duke of Northumberland and the Church of England are paid more for every ton of coal that passes through their estates, than is the man who laboured to dig it from the earth. Where is the justice in that?'

He's a small man, slight and stooped. He looks worn out and his voice is hoarse, but he has the crowd hanging on his every word. When he pauses, a cheer goes up, so loud it makes my ears ring.

'Comrades—the Archbishop of Westminster preaches from his pulpit that our strike is a sin against God. Mr Churchill calls us Bolsheviks and urges the Prime Minister to send troops and armoured cars against us. Our leaders in Labour and the TUC demonstrate daily that their hearts are not with us in our struggle. But we will persist. We must, because we have no other resource. The strike is the worker's only weapon.'

I look around at the faces in the crowd. Bitter, weary faces, fixed on one man with a desperate kind of hope that breaks my heart. Most of these blokes lived through the horror of the trenches, made it back only to be thrown on the waste heap. I swear, I'll fight this rotten system till I die trying.

'Hello, stranger.'

There's a tap on my shoulder and I look up at a familiar face. 'Nora! Bleedin' hell!'

We spent a lot of time together in the old days, fighting for the vote. When the war started and she decided to join the VAD, I was angry with her. I felt betrayed. Like she'd lined up with the other side. Her reasons were complicated, I suppose, and she saw the light in the end. She came back and worked for peace and it didn't take long to forget our differences. Bottom line, we went on our first hunger strike together and you don't forget a thing like that. She was with me and Sylvia Pankhurst and the others on the day we voted for the first time. She's a sister.

'It's been ages!' I say.

'I know. No excuse really. We're only in Ealing.'

She's still got that special smile that comes from nowhere and draws you in.

'I'm glad to see you.'

'Me too.' She nods towards the group on the gallery steps. 'I've come to hear Ellen.'

As if on cue, a little woman stands forward and takes the loud hailer. She has a face like a mischievous imp but no one who knows her is fooled by that. Ellen Wilkinson has a will of iron. She was a Suffragette with Nora in Manchester and now she's a Labour MP and a fierce fighter for the workers. She stands there in front of the massive stone columns, all five foot of her, and a ray of sunshine breaks through the clouds and lights her up as she starts to speak, as if nature was casting a vote for justice.

'I know you feel betrayed and angry and I don't blame you,' she says simply, and it feels like everyone there takes a step towards her. 'There are those in Westminster who should be ashamed to call themselves Labour, who sit in small rooms with Union men and this cold-hearted government, discussing your lives with no real understanding of what you endure. But I want you to know that you are not alone in this struggle. I will fight for you with my last breath. It's a long road, Comrades, but we walk it together.'

There's a moment's silence when she finishes, louder than any cheers. The man next to me, short and stocky in his Sunday suit and polished boots, takes off his cap, like he's paying his respects. There are tears in his eyes. I look at Nora and she squeezes my arm as the applause breaks out in a deafening wave.

'Good for Ellen,' I shout, and she nods.

'We need more like her.'

'And less like Ramsay MacDonald.'

It's hard when your own side let you down. You expect to be betrayed by your enemies but not by your friends. Strikes shouldn't be used as political weapons, my arse. MacDonald will wait a long time to be forgiven and it's no more than he deserves.

I joined the Labour Party because of Keir Hardie. I suppose everyone who joins wants to see a fairer world or they wouldn't bother, but some aren't as hungry for it as they should be. There's plenty in Parliament who think that the crumbs from the rich man's table are all we can hope for and that we have to play their game to get what little they allow us. Compromise, they say. Crumbs are better than nothing. Well, I say bollocks to that. It's war so pick a side.

The crowd starts to break up and Nora takes my arm.

'Fancy a cuppa? Rose and Harry are in a teashop round the corner.'

Nora came back from Gallipoli with a bun in the oven. And with Rose, the love of her life. The two of them run a school in Ealing. The boy has just turned ten now and has two mums, but lots of families have no men these days, so their set-up isn't out of the ordinary and most people don't give it a second thought. Which is handy for them. The theatre has always been live and let live but elsewhere, things ain't so easy going.

We weave our way along the pavement, past St Martin-in-the-Fields to a little café in Adelaide Street where Rose is sitting, plump and pretty, at a table in the window. She gives a wave when she sees us and Harry grins at us over the massive cream bun he's holding in both hands

'We're going to Australia,' he says to me as soon as I sit down.

I look across at Nora and she nods.

'He's never seen his grandparents. It's time they met him.'

'Have they met you?'

'No. I got in touch when Mike was killed. They didn't know I was pregnant. It helped them, I think, to have a bit of him carrying on. We've exchanged photos and letters but never been till now.'

'Well it ain't exactly next door, is it?'

'It's ten thousand miles,' says Harry, through a mouthful of cake. 'It takes five weeks to get there on a ship.'

'Don't speak whilst you're eating,' says Nora, and he grins and licks the crumbs from his lips.

I order afternoon tea and the waitress brings a silver cake

stand loaded with goodies. Lovely little sandwiches with the crusts cut off, fancy cakes and scones with jam and cream. When I was a kid, I used to stare through the steamy windows of places like this and dream of cream eclairs and strawberry tarts. One day, I'd tell myself. One day. Well here I am. Nothing to write home about, granted. Just a teashop. What kind of world do we live in, that it's still out of reach for so many?

'I forgot your dad was Australian,' I say to Harry.

'He died in the war. He had blue eyes like me.'

'And the same cheeky grin.' Nora ruffles his hair and he laughs.

'You all going?' I ask as I reach for a scone.

Rose shakes her head.

'We can't leave the school for that long. I'm holding the reins here.'

'It's a long time.'

'Slaving away whilst we go globe-trotting.' Nora laughs but she reaches for Rose's hand and I see the look that passes between them over their entwined fingers. I don't think they've spent a day apart since they met.

'You'll have to come and keep me company,' Rose says to me.

'Course I will.'

'The girls are putting on a play in August. "Arms and the Man." Maybe you could help us with it?'

'That's a proper play. Not what I'm used to! But I'm happy to help if I can.'

'We'd love it.'

'I'm writing a play,' says Harry.

I'm piling cream on top of jam, but I stop and look across at him.

'What about?'

'Cowboys,' he says solemnly and goes back to his bun.

'Remember when we saw you in pantomime last year?' Nora asks. 'He came home and wrote his own.'

' "Sleeping Beauty and the Pirates",' says Harry.

'Good title.'

'I've written eleven plays. I'm going to be a writer for money when I grow up. Or a train driver.'

Rose and Nora exchange proud smiles over his head and I wonder what it must be like to bring up a kid, to be a mum, to feel that responsibility and consuming love. No, I think, as I lick the jam off my fingers. No, not for me. Politics is my baby. Still, they've done a good job with the boy. I like him.

'Do you fancy seeing "Lady Be Good"?'

'Yes please!' His face lights up.

'Are you sure, Daisy?' asks Nora.

'No problem. I can get you some comps on a weeknight.'

'It's good of you. Say thanks, Harry.'

'Thank you, Daisy.'

'You're welcome.'

Rose is signalling to the waitress for the bill and we're all reaching for hats and coats when there's a sudden commotion out on the street, shouts and police whistles, and we all look round. A bloke flashes by the café window, running hard, with two Special Constables not far behind. Thousands of Specials have been sworn in, to back up the police. Everywhere you look, they're strutting about with their chests puffed out, blowing their bleedin' whistles any chance they get. Bastards. Lots of people don't agree with the strike or don't understand it, but to line up with the government takes a special kind of class traitor, if you ask me. I don't know what the bloke they're chasing has done but I know whose side I'm on. They disappear up the street with a crowd behind them and I jump up and throw some money on the table.

'I'm getting in on this!'

'Solidarity!' Nora calls after me as I run for the door.

'I'll be in touch about the tickets,' I shout over my shoulder and they all wave as I leg it towards the action.

Near the corner, there's a narrow archway leading to a small court of houses and it's blocked by people standing three deep, looking in and laughing. I can't see a bleedin' thing. I try edging to the front but I can't get through.

'What's happening?' I ask a tall bloke next to me and he answers without turning.

'They're trapped,' he says. 'Serve 'em right.'

'They chased him in.' A little girl sitting on the kerb is jiggling a toddler on her knee. She's thin and pale, shivering in the sharp wind.

'Where's your coat?' I ask her.

'Haven't got one. He nipped into one of the houses and now the Specials can't find him.'

I give her my scarf. She wraps it round her and the baby and her sudden smile breaks my heart. I see a gap open up and I squeeze through it till I get a view. The two Specials are standing in the middle of the grimy court, looking nervous. There's no way out but through the crowd and we're not moving, so they're going nowhere. Then I see what everyone's laughing at. The upstairs windows are open all round them and half a dozen women are leaning out, holding chamber pots.

'Where's the fugitive?' one of the Specials shouts. He's short and stocky with bushy eyebrows and thinning hair. I can see the sweat breaking out on his scalp and upper lip. He's nervous but trying to cover it.

'Why do you want him?' a voice shouts from the back.

'He knocked a policeman's helmet off,' says number two. He's thin and wiry and cockier than his mate. 'Hand him over.'

There are hoots from all sides. For fuck's sake. Have they nothing better to do?

'Let 'em have it!' somebody yells, and the crowd roars its approval.

There's movement from the women upstairs, the Specials throw their arms over their heads and bend double and the air is suddenly acrid as a shower of piss rains down on their backs. Everyone round me is laughing and shouting but as the two blokes straighten up, the noise dies down. There's a hunted look in their eyes as they look around them and it isn't funny anymore. In the quiet, the windows above us bang shut, one after another. Some of the crowd look as uncomfortable as I feel, some are still hostile, but there's a slow movement and they part to make a way through to the street. The Specials don't budge at first. They stand like statues, eyeing their escape route nervously and then, all at once, they make a break for it. Next to me, the little girl rests the toddler on one hip and reaches for my hand. Her fingers are freezing. I slip both our hands into my pocket, for warmth, and we stand together without talking, watching the two men scuttle away, the backs of their coats stained dark and wet. I feel weary suddenly. Divide and conquer. That's how they keep us in our place.

*

There are ten of us in the chorus dressing room and there isn't space to swing a cat. I've got a chair and a square foot of counter in front of the blotchy mirror and I can't move without bumping elbows with the girls either side. That's the glamorous West End for you.

The costumes are on a rail running down the middle of the room, divided into ten sections, one for each of us—and woe betide anyone who doesn't put 'em back in the right place, arranged properly on the hanger, or you'll have Flo Wilson to deal with. She's the Wardrobe Mistress, a tiny woman in an old-fashioned black dress with lace at the collar and cuffs. Her bodice is peppered with loose dress pins and needles threaded with a rainbow of different colour threads, just in case, she says. Gawd knows how old she is. I've known her for donkey's years, since my first panto, when I was just a kid, and she looked exactly the same then. Straight back, silver hair in a tight bun and fierce grey eyes that miss absolutely nothing. When she comes into the dressing room before the show, I see Maisie Dunn, the youngster on my right, cast a nervous look at the rail to make sure her stuff is all shipshape, and she's not the only one. You don't cross Flo, if you know what's good for you. She'll have your guts for garters.

There's the usual chatter on all sides, as we put our make-up on, but I don't join in this time. I'm still feeling a bit rattled, if I'm honest, after the business with the Specials. I keep thinking about the desperation under the jeers and laughter and the little girl's cold hand letting go of mine before she carried her baby brother up a crumbling flight of stone steps in the corner. I don't know why I keep picturing that squalid court of houses, I've seen plenty of slums in my time, just as bad and worse. But I can't shake the look on that child's face when I gave her my old scarf. I concentrate on my greasepaint sticks and powder laid out neatly on the square of towel in front of me, breathe in the familiar smells of oil and perfume and try to take comfort in the routine of blending five and nine on my face and dotting carmine on my lips and cheeks. But I still feel low. It's this bleedin' strike, I suppose, making all the injustice scream even louder in my head.

'Penny for 'em.'

Flo is standing behind my chair and our eyes meet in the mirror.

'Alright, Flo?'

'You were miles away.'

'Yeah. Bit of a day.'

'You been out with the Bolshies again, Daisy?' Tilly Potts, on my left, leaves off powdering her nose to smirk into her mirror. Any chance to have a dig, Tilly jumps at it.

I turn and give her my best smile.

'I've been supporting the workers, Tilly, and proud of it.'

'Workers? Working is just what they aren't doing. I had to walk in again today. Not a bus or tram in sight. It's a disgrace.'

'It's solidarity.'

'Bleedin' unions. Troublemakers.'

'Tilly's right,' pipes up old Ethel Maitliss from across the room. Ethel is the character woman and must be seventy if she's a day. She's worked with 'em all and has some great stories to tell. I've a lot of time for her, but her politics are straight out of the bleedin' Daily Mail. God, King and Empire, Amen.

'But what about the miners?' asks little Maisie on my right. 'It isn't fair what's been done to them, is it?'

Tilly is piling her long dark hair on top of her head. She's proud of it. Calls it her crowning glory. No modern bob for Tilly Potts. When she lets it drop, it streams down her back like a black river. She has fine dark eyes too and they're hard as flint when she turns 'em on Maisie.

'Life ain't fair. Sooner those strikers realise that, the better.'

'The country's in debt,' says Ethel. 'We can't spend what we haven't got.'

'It wasn't the poor who got us in debt.'

'But it's the poor who suffer for it.'

'No point striking though. Nothing ever changes.'

'What's the point of unions anyway?'

There are comments flying on all sides. Normally I'd weigh in and set 'em all straight, but, for once, I can't work up the energy. They've heard it all from me before and what good did it do? Water off a duck's back. Tilly has turned back to the mirror and a mouthful of hairpins is keeping her quiet for a bit, so I leave 'em all to it. That's when Flo starts talking and the dressing room goes quiet around her. Watching her in my mirror, I see her pull herself up to her full height, which isn't much, but suddenly she seems taller.

'When I was a corsetmaker, as a girl, I earned a penny for making a corset that sold for a guinea.' Her grey eyes flash around from face to face. 'We had to buy our own needles and thimbles out of that and if the boss didn't consider the corset perfect, we were fined. If we were late to work, we were fined. If we got a cut from the whalebone and bled on the fabric, we were fined. Sometimes the fines took your whole week's wage, twelve hours a day for nothing and nothing we could do about it. Then we formed a Union. No more fines. And tuppence a corset.' She stops and looks straight at Tilly. 'Who do you think the Unions are? They're you and me. They're all of us. Take your head out of your arse, girl. You make me tired.'

And with that, she walks out, leaving everybody staring. Tilly has two pink spots on her cheeks that aren't make-up. She's livid but she hasn't the nerve to cross swords with Flo.

'My dad says Unions are like a bundle of sticks,' says Maisie. 'You can break one stick but bind 'em together and they won't break so easy.'

'They still burn though, don't they?' snaps Tilly.

Maisie looks crestfallen but I give her a wink and she gives me a little smile.

'Five minutes,' shouts the call-boy in the corridor and we all make a move for our costumes.

'Lord Cavendish sent flowers to Adele again,' says Ethel and the conversation turns from politics to romance without missing a beat.

A few of the girls, having sat in silence for the last ten minutes, suddenly perk up and show some interest. Whether or not Adele Astaire marries the second son of the Duke of Devonshire is much more interesting to them than how the rich keep their boots on the necks of the poor. Fuck me, it's depressing.

*

When I come out of the stage door after the show, there's a pony and trap in the alley. I look up and there's Sylvia Pankhurst sitting up top and smiling down at me. My heart lifts at the sight of her. A dose of Sylvia is just what I need right now.

'Your carriage to Camberwell, Madam,' she says, and I climb up and give her a hug.

'You're a sight for sore eyes and no mistake.'

'I've been visiting Humphrey and when he said you were due this evening, I thought a ride would be welcome.'

'It is, thanks. It's a long walk if you don't want to catch a bus driven by a strike-breaker.'

'Even further to Woodford,' she says, as she clicks the horse into motion. 'So I borrowed this from the grocer who, lucky for us, is a good Socialist.'

She lives out at Woodford Wells now, in a ramshackle little place overlooking the green, naming it Red Cottage and scandalising the neighbours by living in sin with an Italian. She doesn't change, and I love the bones of her.

I'm glad she's found someone. When Keir Hardie died, at the start of the war, I thought she'd never smile again. Her mother and sister had already broken her heart, recruiting at rallies and handing out white feathers to men not in uniform.

'Women should be for peace,' she wept on my shoulder when she found out.

And then Mr Hardie destroyed his health, campaigning for peace all over the country and seeing his own people turn against him in their war fever. It was a terrible sad end for such a great man. Sylvia seemed to get smaller after that. She threw herself into her work in the East End, welfare centres, mother and baby clinics, soup kitchens—saving lives through those dark years choked with death.

'Penny for them.' Her voice breaks into my thoughts.

'You're the second person to say that to me tonight.'

'What is it, Daisy?'

I look up into her familiar kind eyes and feel my own fill up with tears, no matter how hard I try to swallow them down. Bleedin' hell. I don't know what's got into me lately. The pony's hooves clip-clop through the quiet streets, rows of houses with lights behind their drawn curtains and smoke curling from their chimneys. People inside having supper maybe, listening to the wireless, getting on with their lives. Ordinary people, doing just well enough to distance themselves from those who aren't so lucky. Closing their eyes and ears and looking after their own.

'We're going to lose this strike, aren't we?'

'It looks that way, yes.'

'And things will be worse, not better.'

I'm angry. Mad as hell. No change there. But what's new, what's eating me up, is I'm scared. For the first time, I'm thinking what we're fighting for might never happen. Never. No matter how long and hard we struggle. I'm ashamed to admit it, to Sylvia of all people. She doesn't know what it is to doubt or falter and I feel like I'm letting her down, this quiet little woman sitting next to me with bottomless courage in her heart.

'How many setbacks did we have?' she asks me. 'How many times did we lose before we won?'

'I know.'

'It's long and mighty work, Daisy. We were handed the torch and others will carry it after we're gone. It's as simple as that.'

We're coming into Camberwell, past The Palace, which used to be Dan Leno's Palace of Varieties when I played it before the war. It mainly shows films now. Milly Winsome might be smiling down from the screen in there soon. When I was on the bill, Joe Elvin was the star comic and he recruited us all into the new union, the Variety Artistes' Federation. The management had introduced matinees—six extra shows a week for no extra pay—and the VAF fought it. We went on strike and we got our money. Just like Flo in her corset factory. Stronger together.

It's been a quiet ride through the dark streets but suddenly there's noise in the distance, a clamour of voices that gets louder as we draw closer.

'What's going on?'

We turn a corner and see a crowd at the bottom of the street, outside the tram depot. In front of them, there's a line of Coppers, truncheons drawn and an officer on horseback trotting up and down behind the ranks, watching the face-off. Since the strike started, the pickets have been preventing the council from getting at the trams. Camberwell has its own strike committee and they've been well organised, holding rallies and printing leaflets. They've got a lot of support round here. I can see a few familiar faces in the crowd, angry faces. The air is crackling with tension. Sylvia stops the pony and we get down and walk towards the trouble. Just like old times.

'You are breaking the law,' the officer on the horse is saying. 'You need to disperse immediately.'

'And you need to piss off!' shouts a woman at the front, small and thin and bristling with a lifetime of pent-up resentment. She throws a look of contempt at a young Constable in the middle of the line. 'You should be ashamed of yourself, Jimmy Wade. Your whole family on strike and you standing there in that uniform, doing the boss's dirty work.'

All eyes turn on Constable Wade. He doesn't move or speak, but under the Copper's helmet, his face flushes deep red.

'That's enough from you,' says the officer. He's plump and shiny, with a condescending manner that puts my back right up. No way is he going to pour oil on troubled waters. There's only one way this is going.

'Am I not allowed to speak now?' The woman turns to the people around her and her voice gets louder. 'This is what we're fighting against. The tyranny of the state!'

There are shouts from all sides.

'You tell him, girl!'

'Big man on a big horse. Get down and face us, I dare you.'

'That's right. He daren't.'

Me and Sylvia have reached the edges of the crowd, near the police horse, which is bigger and more threatening close up, the muscles rippling under its shiny black coat and its hooves loud on the cobbled street. The line of Coppers draws tight together as the tension rises and I feel it in my bones, the old mix of fear and excitement. I look at Sylvia and I can see it's the same for her.

'It's going to kick off any minute.'

She nods and calls up to the mounted policeman.

'Officer. Let me speak to them.'

He looks down at her like she's just crawled out from under a stone. He has no idea who she is. Too young to have been in the force when we were being arrested on a regular basis. All he sees is a plain little woman getting above herself. Too young to have fought in the war too, I'd say, or he'd have less appetite for confrontation.

'I can calm them,' she says, and I know she could, given the chance, but she ain't getting it.

'You have no right to impede access to the trams,' he shouts, ignoring her. 'Stand aside or suffer the consequences.'

There's a noise from the crowd, like a low growl. They move back in a mass, blocking the depot doors. The Coppers tighten their grip on the truncheons.

'Advance!' raps the officer and the line moves forward.

A few men have positioned themselves at the front of the crowd but, as the police approach, the small woman pushes through and stands like a rock, face to face with Constable Wade.

'Come on then, Jimmy,' she says quietly. 'You're not getting by me, so you'll have to go through me.'

For a breathless second, the Copper looks her in the eye and I think, he won't, he can't, but then he raises his arm and brings the truncheon down on her and, as she cries out, I watch his face. It goes from red to white, goes hard and blank. He lifts the truncheon again and I can't help myself, I move forward to stop him somehow, to save her, get her away. But I've only taken a step when he goes down under a rush of blokes, punching and kicking and he's on the ground, curled in a ball, trying to squirm clear. Then the other Coppers pile in and all hell breaks loose. It's just a scrum of bodies and shouting and hate and fear.

At my side, Sylvia turns to the mounted officer, her face desperate.

'You could have prevented this!'

He looks down at her and he smiles. He smiles. The fucker. I'm wondering how hard it would be to pull him off that bleedin' horse when there's whistles and running feet and dozens more Coppers come at us from all directions. Reinforcements. It'll soon be over now. As they launch in, I see the little woman move clear of the fight and I grab her arm. There's tears running through the blood on her face and she keeps saying, 'I've known him all his life. All his life.'

Sylvia gives me a look and I nod. There's nothing we can do here. Better to get at least one of them out of it, before the trouble dies down, before the Coppers take stock and make arrests. We walk her down the street and into the pony and trap. She lets us take her away but she's still crying when we get to Humph's house and take her inside.

Her name is Mary Jackson and she's a washerwoman with six kids. Her husband is a striking bus driver and none of 'em have had a decent meal for a week, not that they lived on the fat of the land when he was earning. They scraped a living and, of course, they had nothing put by. There's never any spare when you live hand to mouth. But no way would Ernie Jackson break the strike. He came from a family of miners and knew what it was to slave in the dark all day for a pittance. He'd never betray them.

'He's with 'em heart and soul,' she says. 'And he's right.'

Humph has brought a bowl of warm water and a cloth from the kitchen and he's sitting beside her at the table in the parlour, wiping the blood and tears from her face. He's so gentle. When he dabs the cut on her forehead and she winces, he gives her hand a little squeeze.

'Not much longer,' he tells her.

Just like the old days, when I was on release after a hunger strike and weak as a kitten, or when I'd been knocked about a bit at a demonstration. He's a safe harbour. I bet he was the same in the trenches. How many terrified eyes did he look into? How many dying hands did he hold? They're all still there in his head, haunting his dreams. I wish I could take the burden from him. He did it for me often enough.

'Here we are.' Sylvia comes in with a tray of tea. 'Hot and sweet. Drink it down.'

Humph has finished with the cloth and put a sticking plaster on the cut.

'All done.'

'You're kind. You've all been very kind.'

'You were very brave,' says Sylvia.

'I was just so mad, I didn't think.'

'Where have I heard that before?' asks Humph, giving me a wink.

'He grew up next door to us.' Mary shakes her head, bewildered. 'Jimmy. He played football with my eldest. His dad and brothers are on the buses. Out on strike. I never thought—'

'It's a steady job, the police force,' says Sylvia. 'Tempting in hard times.'

'I get that. But on nights like tonight, you have to choose a side, don't you?'

Couldn't have put it better myself. Mary puts down her cup and stands up.

'I've got to get back home. Ernie'll be wondering where I've got to. I only nipped out to pick up a wash load, but I saw the crowd at the depot—if he's heard about the trouble, he'll be worried—he can't leave the kids—'

'I'll take you.' Sylvia gets to her feet.

'It's alright.'

'Let's get you home.'

'You've done enough.'

'Not at all.'

'I can do it,' says Humph.

Ever the gentleman. But Sylvia's having none of it.

'The pony knows me. I won't be long.'

We see them out and wave them off, watching until they turn the corner and the sound of hooves fades into the night. I see Humph has a crease of worry between his eyes as we close the door and I give his arm a squeeze.

'They'll be fine.'

'There could still be trouble on the streets.'

'Sylvia can look after herself.'

'True enough.'

We've already planned that she'll stay the night with us so Humph satisfies himself by lighting a fire in the spare room and putting a hot water bottle in her bed before she comes back.

Down in the parlour, I sit in a chair by the hearth and toast my toes. It's been a long day and I'm shattered. I watch the flames curling up the chimney, breathe in the comforting smell of soot and smoke, plump up the cushion behind my back and have a little wallow in small pleasures. There's a big poster on the wall by the window. Humphrey Carter and his Celebrated Dogs. Matthew, Mark, Luke and John. He sold 'em on when he enlisted and says he still misses 'em. When he gets misty-eyed about 'em and I take the piss, he shakes his head at me and spreads out his arms.

'Look around you, girl,' he says. 'They bought this place, those dogs. We've a lot to thank 'em for.'

It washes over me, suddenly, how right he is and how much I love this little house, full of Humph's bits and pieces, smelling faintly of his shaving soap, a memory in every corner. It's home. The only place I've ever thought of in that way. Life can be a struggle. The theatre, the war, the fight for the vote and for justice. I wouldn't have it different, I can't imagine not striving for something, but we all need somewhere to rest, someone to hold.

The door opens and Humph comes in. He sits in his chair, opposite mine, and gives me a smile and I think of that bit in *Far from the Madding Crowd* where Gabriel Oak says, '*When you look up, there shall I be and when I look up, there shall you be.*' Something like that, anyway. I love that book.

'Alright, girl?' Humph asks.

It's just a greeting. A sign of affection. He doesn't expect an answer. But I lean forward and look into his face in the firelight.

'I think we should get married,' I say.

1936

TWO deaths today. The King and my old life. I saw the billboards on my way to Ealing. His Majesty had died during the night and the newsboys were shouting on every corner. 'The Nation Grieves.' Does it? I didn't expect there would be much mourning where I was going.

I told my parents I was having tea at Claridges with cousin Vera. It was another deceit but they didn't suspect a thing. We always went to Claridges on my birthday and today I was eighteen and considered old enough to go without them. I was sorry I had to lie but they simply wouldn't understand the truth.

'I know where our money comes from and I can't bear it—'

No. I couldn't tell them that. I was too afraid of the consequences. I was still trying to live in two worlds, delaying the inevitable, walking the tightrope and waiting for the fall.

*

The Paget School for Girls is a big, old house in its own grounds, overlooking Ealing Common. It was a grand home once, with curving staircases, marble fireplaces and stained-glass windows, but now the wooden floors and doors are scuffed and battered and there are desks and blackboards in the high-ceilinged rooms. On my first visit, Harry gave me a tour and, in some ways, it reminded me of the school I went to; I suppose all Common Rooms and dormitories are much the same. But that's where the similarity ends. I was taught that God is in his heaven and all is right with the world, that the future for me was debutante balls, a good marriage, an heir and a spare. The Paget girls are luckier. They get a real education.

I walked up the drive, past the little Lodge where Harry lived now, and round to the side door. It was a bright, cold day and the grass in the shade under the trees was still rimed with frost. There were drifts of snowdrops in the borders and a few early crocuses pushing through, in bright spots of purple and yellow. I felt alive with happiness to be there, to be invited and accepted. And because I would see Harry.

Rose answered the bell and greeted me with a smile.

'Happy Birthday!'

She ushered me into the kitchen where Nora was at the stove, brewing tea. It was a small, cosy room in their private quarters, away from the bustle of the main school. Our kitchen at home was Cook's ordered domain and I rarely set foot in it, but this room was different, it was warm and welcoming. There was a woman I didn't know sitting at the table. She looked older than Rose and Nora, with vivid red hair and a pretty face.

'This is Daisy,' Nora put the teapot down beside her. 'And this is the birthday girl.'

'Glad to meet you,' Daisy smiled.

'We're old comrades,' said Nora. 'Pull up a chair, Charlotte. Make yourself at home.'

'Thank you for giving me tea,' I said. 'It's very kind.'

'You're more than welcome.' Rose pushed a small box across the table. 'This is for you.'

It was a brooch. A small flag in red enamel for my lapel.

'For when your secret's out,' said Nora.

'Thank you. It's lovely.'

'Any closer to telling them?'

I shook my head.

'Rose had the same problem,' said Daisy.

'Did you?'

'A progressive school for girls? My family were appalled. I tried to explain that there was no going back to my old life after the war. They didn't understand.'

'Harry told me you and Nora were nurses.'

'On Lemnos. For casualties from Gallipoli.'

'It's where we met,' said Nora.

The two of them shared a smile. Rose is as fair as Nora is dark and a head shorter. She comes from a life very similar to mine. When I look at her I see what's possible and it gives me hope. Nora still has her Lancashire accent, though she hasn't

99

lived there for years. She was a mill girl before the war, before she and Rose met. There's a strength about Nora, as solid as the hills. That's where Harry gets it from. His mother is a force of nature.

Daisy got to her feet.

'I'd better get a move on.'

'Not staying for cake?'

'I've got an early show.'

'Daisy's in the revue at The Hippodrome,' said Rose.

'For my sins. I can get you tickets but I wouldn't recommend it. It's bleedin' rubbish. But what can you do?'

She was what my parents would call rough and ready, if they were feeling kind. They would be bewildered that I wanted to be here. I could picture the looks on their faces as Daisy hugged Rose and Nora and turned to pat my shoulder.

'Happy Birthday, ducks. See you again.'

There was a rush of cold air as she went out, then the door closed behind her.

'The show isn't that bad,' Rose laughed. 'Well, actually it is, but Daisy is always worth watching.'

'I've never met an actress before. This new life is full of surprises.'

'There's all sorts in the Labour Party,' said Nora. 'Life's rich tapestry!'

She was right. I don't know what I expected when I walked into the hall for my first meeting. Lots of cloth caps and shouting, if I'm honest, but otherwise, I didn't have a clue. The caps are there, of course, but so are Oxbridge scarves and lots of women and youngsters. Apparently, all kinds of people want to change the world.

'Did your family understand in the end?' I asked Rose.

'Not really. They've learnt to tolerate it.'

It wasn't the answer I wanted to hear.

'But it's a wonderful school. It's making a difference.'

'That's the plan,' said Nora.

'When Harry said he grew up in a girls' school, I thought he was joking.'

'Did I hear my name?' said a voice from the doorway.

Nora smiled the smile she saves for him. I turned and there he was—untidy dark hair, bright blue eyes behind his round glasses and a big grin when he saw me. He held out a bunch of red tulips.

'Happy Birthday.'

'Thank you.' My heart turned over. He brought me flowers.

Rose went to the pantry and emerged a few seconds later carrying a cake with eighteen flickering candles.

'Harry said chocolate was your favourite. Quick. Make a wish.'

They sang 'Happy Birthday' as I blew out the candles. Let it be more than friends I wished, let it happen. Could he see in my face how much I love him? Ever since that first day when I sat at the back of the meeting and he spoke from the platform straight to my heart, I've known that he is the lost half of me. I can't contain it, love just spills out of me whenever I see him.

After his third slice of cake, Harry looked over his shoulder to where Nora and Rose were washing dishes at the sink, then he smiled at me.

'Come into the hall for a minute.'

I followed him out of the room. He was standing by the stairs, where he had dropped his jacket and bag on the way in, holding a small brown paper parcel.

'I got you this.'

A pocket-sized book. Shelley's poems, bound in soft, red leather.

'It's beautiful.'

'He's my favourite poet. He said poets are the unacknowledged legislators of the world.'

'I love it. Thank you.'

When I looked up, there was something new in his eyes, something that sucked the air from my lungs. The sun was striking through the stained glass in the window, casting coloured patterns on the floor, like rainbows at our feet. Dust motes were dancing in a shaft of light between us. I felt vividly aware of every sound, every movement, like I was living in slow motion.

And the sunlight clasps the earth, and the moonbeams kiss the sea.
What is all this sweet work worth, if thou kiss not me?

His voice was low and close. I couldn't speak. I could barely breathe. He leaned in and kissed me softly, his lips on mine for the briefest, longest time.

101

'Happy Birthday,' he whispered, and I felt the warmth of his breath on my cheek.

I had closed my eyes; I don't know why. To contain the moment perhaps, to control my pounding heart and whirling brain. When I opened them, he was smiling down at me and I wondered that such happiness was possible. I reached up and touched his face with my fingers.

'He was a womaniser,' I said. 'Shelley.'

'He was.'

'A breaker of hearts.'

He wrapped my fingers in his and looked at me solemnly.

'I'll never break yours. I promise.'

When he bent to me again, I sought out his mouth greedily and there was nothing in the world but our two bodies pressed together and our urgent kisses. I don't know how much time passed before the kitchen door swung open and we pulled apart as Nora appeared in the hall.

'I'm making more tea. Want a cup?'

'Lovely.' Harry spoke to her, but he was still looking at me.

'Two minutes. Then you can tell me how the play's coming on.'

She retraced her steps. We stood face to face for a moment, then followed her. I felt newly self-conscious with Nora and Rose but they carried on as normal. Why wouldn't they? It was my life, not theirs, that had just been transfigured.

'Did you know Harry was writing a play, Charlotte?' Nora was pouring the tea. 'It's about his great-great grandmother Hannah. She was imprisoned for riot and disturbance.'

'She was a handloom weaver,' said Rose. 'When the mechanised looms came in, they were left behind and left to starve. So they tried to destroy the machines.'

Harry laughed. 'I come from a long line of convicts.'

'Political prisoners, if you please.' Nora rapped his knuckles with her teaspoon.

'Ow! Sorry.'

Rose saw my curiosity and put her hand over Nora's on the table, part protective, part proud.

'Nora was a Suffragette,' she told me.

'I'm not surprised.'

'That I'm a jailbird?'

'That you put up a fight.'

'Well there was a fight the day I was arrested, that's for sure.'

'The police raided a meeting where Sylvia Pankhurst was speaking.'

I stared in awe. Sylvia Pankhurst was my idol. She was everything I wanted to be.

'I went prepared,' Nora laughed. 'We used to pack our clothes with cardboard for when the Bobbies got violent.'

'The police attacked you?'

'All the time.'

'Weren't you terrified?'

'Not at first, no. Everything happened so fast it didn't seem real. It was only when we were sent down and I saw the walls of Holloway, I sobered up. I was scared then right enough.'

'She went on hunger strike.' Harry's voice was full of pride.

'We all did. That was the routine. That's when I first met Daisy.'

'She was a Suffragette too?'

'She was a legend in the movement and no wonder—practically lived in Holloway.'

'You've met Daisy?' Harry asked me.

'She was here earlier.'

'She wants to see your play,' said Nora.

'It isn't finished yet.'

'She says is there a part for her?'

'There could be. Good old Daisy.'

'We cast our first votes together after the war.' Nora held out her hand. 'She gave me this ring.'

'It's an aquamarine,' I said.

'That's right. For courage.'

'Speaking of which,' said Rose. 'Time to go public, Harry.'

'It's nowhere near ready.'

'We always read your plays.'

'But this one is different. It feels different.'

'Come on, son,' said Nora. 'Bite the bullet.'

He looked from one of them to the other.

'Alright,' he sighed. 'You win.'

'Of course.'

Taking a notebook from his overflowing bag, he flicked through the pages.

'Here's a song from Act One. It needs work—but, here.'

He laid the open book on the table and we all bent our heads to read it.

The Progress Song

I learned a trade at my father's knee.
I learned a craft at my mother's side.
Riches were for luckier folk,
We had food and fuel and a craftsman's pride.
We made cloth, we earned a living
By the sweat of an honest brow.
I could hold my head high, I was a weaver
But what am I fit for now?

The government says it's progress,
It's for the common good.
Resistance would be pointless.
They wouldn't if they could.
For Industry must have its day,
This is the march of man.
And those who fall along the way
Must do the best they can.

The machines are a hundred times faster
And running them is cheap
When you can hire unskilled labour
And children half-asleep.
And as long as the profits are rolling in,
Who cares for the human cost?
Who grieves for the end of an era?
Who mourns for what is lost?

The government says it's progress.
The price we have to pay.
For England's tomorrow,
We must give our today.

And the villages die,
And the handlooms are still,
And we bury our children

In the shadow of the mill.
And I try to see a future
But I don't know how.
I was born and bred a weaver
But what am I fit for now?

I looked up from the page and met his eyes. He gave me a nervous smile and my heart swelled for him. I was so proud of the anger and hope that drove him, the fight that bound us together.

'I love it,' I said.

'I want the truth.'

'That is the truth.'

Nora leaned over and ruffled his hair.

'You're doing Hannah proud.'

'Passing it on,' said Rose.

He has two mothers, I thought, as I watched them. How lucky he is to be loved so much, to have nothing to be ashamed of, nothing to explain. Sitting with the three of them, I felt connected to everything that matters and I knew it was where I belonged, that something momentous had happened to me. Whatever the consequences, there was no going back.

*

I was late home and had to change in a hurry, arriving in the drawing room just before dinner.

'Happy Birthday, Sis,' said Miles as I walked in. 'Sorry I missed you this morning. I slept in.'

'Another late night?' Father frowned.

'Late supper with the chaps. You know how it is.'

'Do I?'

Miles laughed. 'Even you were young once, Pa. Shall we have a birthday cocktail?'

'I think not.'

'Not today, Miles,' said Mother. 'I'm sorry, Charlotte darling. I know it's your birthday but the news—' she broke off, near to tears.

For a moment I stared blankly, then I remembered. The King was dead and though it had barely touched my afternoon in Ealing, it was sombre news here at home.

'That's alright,' I sat next to Miles on the sofa.

'Funny to think of a new king, isn't it?' he said. 'Wonder how the next chap will measure up?'

'By doing his duty.' Father gave him a disapproving look, but he wasn't squashed.

'It will be a fair old change for him. Likes the high life, the jolly old Prince of Wales.' He gave me a wink. Miles thinks it's clever to be flippant. He'll never grow up. But then, he'll never have to. 'He'll have less time for Mrs Simpson and the south of France at any rate.'

'He's your king now,' said Father. 'Show some respect.'

He glared into his drink and the firelight sparkled in the cut glass. I thought of Harry's kisses and felt a million miles from Cadogan Square. I looked at my family, dressed for dinner by Savile Row and Paris, and I thought of my tea party and my comrades and what they would think of us, indulged and complacent in our ivory tower. Mother was dabbing at her eyes with a Chantilly handkerchief. Just a scrap of lace. But such expensive, beautifully laundered lace. How strange that such a little thing finally tipped the balance. I remembered some lines from Harry's speech that first day I met him, about how there should be no gold on the king's carriage and no lace on the dress of the duchess when even one poor person was hungry, and the words were out before I could stop them.

'Respect should be earned, shouldn't it?'

They all turned to look at me. Three pairs of eyes full of the same surprise.

'What do you mean?' asked Mother.

'He's a spoilt playboy. Why should I respect that?'

'Charlotte!'

I don't remember getting up but I was on my feet facing them, with my heart hammering in my chest.

'The Royal Family are a living symbol of everything that's wrong with this country. It's time we abolished the monarchy once and for all.'

There was a stunned silence. Miles looked at me with some sympathy, not for my politics of course, but for my predicament. Mother and Father were utterly lost for words. I don't know how long we would have stood there, staring at each other, if

106

Mary hadn't appeared in the doorway and announced dinner was served. Mother was the first to find her voice.

'Give Cook our apologies, Mary. We shall be late this evening.'

'Yes, Ma'am.' She bobbed a curtsey and left. I watched her go and thought how odd it was that she had been there when my world rearranged itself, yet she had no idea.

'What on earth—' Father began but I interrupted him.

'I followed her on her afternoon off. Mary. I followed her.'

The servants had rooms on the top floor but, once a week, she went home to see her family. Mary, who makes our fires and serves our tea. Mary, whom I never imagined having a life without her white lace cap and apron.

I had trailed her through the winter streets, feeling clever and fearless, enjoying my adventure. We walked through parts of London I had never seen before—darker and dingier. The faces we passed were weary, even hostile. I was vividly aware of my shiny shoes and fur-collared coat, of the money in my purse. We turned into a dark alley and my courage nearly failed me, but I walked on until Mary stopped and knocked at a door in the corner of a squalid court of houses. It opened, and she went inside. I stood like stone in the shadow of a filthy wall, breathing fetid air, feeling sick and cold. There was a little boy poking at a puddle with a slimy stick. His ragged trousers were too large and his sweater too small. His boots had no laces and one of them flapped open at the toe showing me a small, dirty foot. His nose was running. I watched him for a long time. I was waiting. When Mary came out again, I stepped forward, into view. She looked at me, surprised and none too pleased. It was wrong that I was there. An invasion. I understood that at last.

'Miss Charlotte?'

'I wanted to see Grandfather's buildings.'

I saw what she thought of me, what was behind her eyes. It had probably always been there but I saw it now.

'Well, this is them, Miss. Your family own the whole lot.'

The little boy dropped his stick and walked past us into the shadows further along the street and, whilst my world shifted on its axis, Mary smiled her servant's smile.

'You better be getting home, Miss Charlotte. It's late.'

I ran away. I ran home. My great adventure ended in a haze of shame and self-loathing. At dinner I couldn't eat a thing and invented a headache to get away to my room. I sat on my bed and wept. I was crying for the little boy with the stick, for Mary, for all the people in all the wretched streets everywhere, but mostly I was crying for myself and my lost content, for the easy life I'd known that was impossible now.

'I followed her to Old Nichol Street.' My family were looking at me as if we were strangers, as if the rug on the floor between us was a bottomless chasm that none of us could cross. 'Grand-father's buildings are slums. Terrible places.' I wasn't angry any more. Just resolute. 'We live off other people's misery.'

'Don't be naive,' said Father. 'There are far worse buildings than ours in London.'

His tone was dismissive. He's right of course, there are worse, I've seen them since then. Streets full of exhausted women and sullen men, small children with old eyes in their young faces. I've seen dying babies, too hungry to cry. I know there are worse buildings than ours, I know that most rich people live off the backs of the poor, but Old Nichol Street opened my eyes and I can't close them again even if I wanted to.

Father stepped to the bell pull and gave it a sharp tug.

'This conversation is at an end,' he said firmly. 'Miles, put down that decanter, Annabel, calm yourself. We shall go into dinner, drink to Charlotte's birthday and hear no more of her nonsense.'

'It isn't—'

'That's enough.'

'You can't simply dismiss it—'

'I can and I do.'

'I can't live this life any more,' I said. 'I have to be of use. I have to do something.'

'Oh, Charlotte,' said Mother. 'No-one expects you to do any-thing.'

No-one expects you to do anything.

I didn't go into dinner. I ignored Father's orders and Mother's tears and ran up to my room. I locked the door and stood with my back to it for a long time, looking at all my fa-miliar things, my books and pictures and childhood dolls. I stood in front of the mirror, looking for changes in my face, for evidence of the new person I've become. I touched my lips softly and my hunger for Harry swelled like a river in flood.

There's no going back now. I have to make plans. I've been pushed off the high wire.

MAY 3RD

We took the girls for a walk today. I was at the back, keeping the stragglers together as we crossed the Common. The sun was shining but there was a cold wind driving the clouds across the sky and bending the swathes of daffodils almost to the ground. A flock of gulls had followed the tidal river inland and landed in patches of stark white below the trees. On the stretch of grass beyond the path, a man was playing fetch the stick with his dog, its excited yelps cutting through the hubbub of chatter from the girls walking ahead of me.

I'm a teaching assistant now. I get a room, my meals and a small salary. Rose insisted. A fair week's pay for a fair week's work, she said, and Nora nodded her approval. As well as Rose and Nora, there are three full-time teachers and me, with thirty-two girls aged twelve to sixteen. A few of them look every bit as old as I do and most of them have seen a lot more. I often feel they should be supervising me and not the other way around.

'You've saved my life,' I told Rose. 'I'm very grateful.'

'We're happy to have you here. You're doing a brave thing, Charlotte.'

'I don't feel brave. Most of the time I'm afraid.'

'But you carry on anyway. That's what courage is.' She squeezed my hand. 'Just put one foot in front of the other. That's what Nora says, and it works.'

So that's what I try to do. I haven't been back to the house in Cadogan Square. I haven't seen my parents for months. When I left, they looked at me with incomprehension and reproach. They think I'm foolish and wrongheaded. I think they are wilfully blind to the cost of their pampered lives. I don't know if we'll ever forgive each other.

I see Miles from time to time. Mother and Father don't know but we meet at a Lyons Corner House and stare at each other over tea and scones whilst I try to make him understand. No, not understand, I try to make him care. But it's no use. He's untouched by the real world and feels no need to connect with it. We take turns at paying the bill and we go our separate ways.

'I like your coat, Miss. It's lovely.'

Little Annie Parker looked back at me from the middle of the group. She has a cheeky grin, an exceptional brain and three younger brothers living in two damp rooms with her parents in Mile End. Nora found her working a cinema queue, doing mental arithmetic tricks for pennies. Now she has a free education and a new life ahead of her. Changing the world one girl at a time, says Rose.

'Thank you, Annie. Don't walk backwards, you'll trip.'

Nora and Rose, leading the way, came to a stop at the edge of the Common where it borders the Broadway. We gathered around them as Nora nodded towards the shop-lined street.

'Looks peaceful today, doesn't it? Ten years ago, hundreds of men marched down there behind a brass band. The General Strike had failed and they were going back to work but they went with heads held high.'

'Bloodied but unbowed,' said Ellen Procter, who couldn't read or write when she arrived but, these days, never has her head out of a book.

'Why did they strike, Miss?' Annie called from the back.

'To support the miners. The coal owners wanted to pay them less money for working more hours. Do you think that's fair?'

'Were the owners getting less money too, Miss?'

'What do you think?'

Annie sniffed.

'Pigs might fly.'

'Why did they lose?' asked Grace Evans, her best friend, as quiet as Annie was lively.

Marjorie Jarvis, a tall, chestnut-haired beauty, pointed at the spire of St Matthew's across the road.

'The church preached that the strike was a sin,' she said. 'The police broke up protesting crowds with baton charges and the middle classes came out in droves to help the government break the strikers.'

Marjorie's father was a radical lawyer and she was planning to be the first woman judge in the country. Grace looked up at her and frowned.

'So it was all for nothing.'

'Fighting for justice is never for nothing,' said Nora. 'You get knocked back but you keep trying. That's how we got Trade

Unions in the first place. It's how women got the vote. It's how everything worth having is won in the end.'

I watched her inspiring those girls, feeding their dreams. A newsboy was shouting today's headlines on the corner—Moseley's Blackshirts were planning another rally in the East End, Hitler's troops had marched into the Rhineland, Mussolini's army was occupying Abyssinia and, in Spain, the Popular Front Government was under attack from Franco's Nationalists. Fascism was spreading like a plague but, on Ealing Common, Nora had the undivided attention of thirty girls learning not to take no for an answer.

*

At teatime, the girls were led back to the school, but I stayed behind because I had the evening off and I was seeing Harry. There was a League of Youth meeting in Dorset Hall at six but, before then, we had an hour in the afternoon sunshine and I was meeting him on our special bench in a secluded corner of the Common. These were the times I treasured. We spend most of our leisure hours campaigning and I love the life but, most of all, I love being alone with him, in his arms, having him all to myself.

He was waiting for me, head bent over his notebook, the breeze playing with his hair. I sat beside him and he looked up.

'Hello, you.'

'How was work?' I asked.

He was apprenticed to a radical printer in Acton, producing pamphlets and papers for every left-wing group in West London. He was in his element.

'Inky,' he smiled. 'How was the walk?'

'Inspiring. Your mother is inspiring.'

'You should meet my gran. The mighty Grace Barnes.'

'Runs in the family then?'

'I hope so.'

I kissed him.

'I know so.'

He closed the book and started to put it away, but I put out a hand to stop him.

'What?'

'Let me read it.'

'Now?'

'I've only seen one song. I want to see more.'

'We've got to go soon.'

'A few pages, at least. The beginning.'

'Really?'

'Yes, really! It's your work.'

'It's my hobby.'

'It's your heart's work. I want to share it.'

'Next time.'

'That's what you always say.'

'I do, don't I?' He hesitated, then gave in and handed it over. On the cover he had written ' "One Foot in Front of the Other" — A play by Harry Barnes'.'

'That's what Nora says,' I remembered.

'That's right. It started with Lizzie.'

'Who?'

'You'll see.'

I leaned back, nestled in the crook of his arm, opened the book and read.

A CELL IN LANCASTER CASTLE — 1826.

(It is dim, cold, cramped and comfortless. Lizzie is lying on a rough bench. Hannah is reading a Bible.)

HANNAH: *"He has filled them with skill to do all kinds of work in blue, purple and scarlet yarn and fine linen." It's here! God made us weavers. It's His will we work at the loom. So why does He take our work away and leave us to starve?*

LIZZIE: *Hush now, Hannah love.*

HANNAH: *What will happen to Clara? What will happen to my little girl?*

LIZZIE: *You'll be back with her soon.*

HANNAH: *She was crying for food and I had nothing to give her. I'd kept her asleep as long as I could. I'd hung a blanket at the window to keep the night in and I rocked her and sang her favourite song and stroked her hair but she wouldn't sleep. She was hungry and there was nothing in the house. Not a scrap. I couldn't stand to hear her. It*

	was like a knife in my heart.
LIZZIE:	*Hush now. Come and sit with me.*
	(She makes room on the bench and Hannah joins her.)
	Will you read something for me?
	(Lizzie shows her a scrap of paper.)
	It's poetry. About Peterloo. Where Sam was killed. I've heard it read, but not for a long time.
	(Hannah takes the paper and reads.)
HANNAH:	*Men of England, heirs of glory,*
	Heroes of forgotten story,
	Nurslings of one mighty mother
	Born of her and one another;
	Rise like lions after slumber
	In unvanquishable number;
	Shake your chains to earth, like dew,
	Which in sleep had fallen on you.
	Ye are many, they are few.
LIZZIE:	*Thank you.*

I looked up from the page.

'Shelley.'

'Our poet.' He smiled and kissed the top of my head.

'Who was Sam?'

'Lizzie's husband. She saw him die. The militia rode into a peaceful protest and killed fifteen people.'

His arm was round my shoulder, his hand stroking my arm as I read on.

HANNAH:	*Will you tell me about Peterloo? Can you bear it?*
	(Lizzie nods. A pause before she speaks.)
LIZZIE:	*Sam and me were in the middle of the Field, listening to the speakers on the platform. Suddenly there was screaming and the horses' hooves like thunder. There was nowhere to run. I grabbed at Sam and he pulled me close to him for a second. I could hear his heart beating fit to burst and then I was on the ground, cowering with my head in my arms, like a frightened child. When I opened my eyes the field was strewn with caps and bonnets—even shoes—all torn and trampled; there were people*

> standing dazed and bloody, people weeping and the
> militia wiping their sabres, walking among the broken
> bodies of the wounded and the dead.

HANNAH: *And Sam?*

LIZZIE: *A few feet away with his head broken open.*

HANNAH: *Oh Lizzie—how did you bear it?*

LIZZIE: *I put one foot in front of the other until the darkness
lifted. It took a while but here I am.*
(She takes the paper back.)
*Men of England it says, but I think it means women as
well, don't you?*

HANNAH: *I think it does.*

LIZZIE: *I'd like to read this for myself. There's a lot of things I'd
like to read. Will you teach me?*

'You could play Hannah,' Harry said. 'Would you like to?'

'What?'

'The League are putting it on in October.'

I sat up and faced him.

'Your play? This play?'

'Yes.'

'Harry! Why didn't you tell me?'

'I just did.'

'How long have you known?'

'Only this morning.' He laughed. 'Have you been in a play
before?'

'Only in school.'

'That's alright. It's all amateurs. It will go on here first, then
go up north for a week or two. Labour Halls and the like—nothing fancy. You'll see where my mum comes from.'

My heart was singing.

'I'd love to do it. But only if you still think I'm right for it when
I've auditioned, like everyone else.'

'No unearned privilege, eh?'

'That's right.'

'Well I don't think there'll be a queue for parts, but, alright,
we'll do it your way.'

'I'm so proud of you.'

I kissed him and he pulled me close.

'I love you, Charlotte West.'

114

'I love you, Harry Barnes.'

'That's lucky then.'

Just then, there was a shout behind us.

'Stop canoodling you two. You're needed.'

It was Tom Willis from the League, a gentle giant, big and broad as a rugby player but brim full of easy-going good nature. He was an Old Etonian and a Cambridge rowing blue, the sort of young man my parents would approve of. Except he was a fervent Socialist and, of course, that would never do.

'Sorry to interrupt, old beans.'

'What's up?'

'Bad news. The summer conference is cancelled.'

'What?' Harry jumped up. 'But it's all organised—'

'Not anymore.' Tom frowned. 'Orders from on high.'

'But why?' I looked at them both, mystified and disappointed. We had worked so hard to put it all together.

'They say we're being infiltrated by Communists.'

'But that's nonsense. The Young Communists have their own group. We're Labour.'

'Better get to the Hall,' said Harry.

Our private time was clearly over. I gave him back the notebook.

'I love it,' I told him. 'I'm proud of you.'

I reached out to touch his face and he kissed my fingers.

'Come on, lovebirds,' said Tom, setting off across the grass. 'There's work to do.'

*

The Hall was filling up when we got there and it was obvious the news had spread quickly. There were dismayed expressions and raised voices. Sally West, the branch secretary, spotted us and raised an arm. Small, ginger and fierce, she was shop steward at the Hoover factory, the youngest ever. Her freckled face was full of anger as she cut through the crowd towards us.

'You need to speak, Harry,' she said. 'We're all downhearted. We need a morale boost.'

'I could do with one myself.'

'Come on, old tulip,' Tom grabbed his arm. 'You're the man for the job.'

Harry allowed himself to be pulled to the front.

'Communist infiltration,' I said to Sally. 'It's ridiculous.'

'It's desperate. Can't they find a new tune to sing?'

'What are they so afraid of?'

'Socialism,' she said bitterly.

Tom was on the stage, asking for order, and the hum of voices quietened.

'Comrades,' he said, 'a few words from Harry Barnes.'

Harry climbed the short run of steps from the floor of the hall and looked out at the faces turned towards him in expectation. He had stood in the same spot when I saw him speak for the first time. It was where he had stolen my heart. It was where he became the best of us, eloquent and full of hope. If anyone could cheer the room, it was him.

'Brothers and Sisters,' his voice rang out, 'there is a great divide in the Labour Party. The hierarchy are hostile towards the League because we challenge them to remember the principles upon which the party was founded.'

There was a murmur of assent from his audience. The evening sun was streaming through the windows, lighting up the peeling plaster and scarred wooden floor. Our meeting place wasn't at all glamorous, but it was alive with a spirit of shared purpose. Among the people gathered in that room, I had found a place to stand in the world. I felt strong. And more than anyone else, Harry was the source of that strength, the well-spring of my courage. I wanted nothing more than a future with him, fighting for a better world, a lifetime of days by his side and nights in his arms.

He moved forward to the very edge of the stage and held out his hands, and it was as if he had reached out to me alone and pulled me close.

'Comrades—Socialism will make no progress in such cautious hands. We will not be cowed and we will not be silenced. Because we know that there is a greater enemy than our own party and we will not be distracted from the great struggle against power and profit. We will persist. And it is from the sparks of groups like this that the mighty flame of Socialism will be lit.'

There was a second of silence then thunderous applause and loud cheers. Tom jumped on the platform to slap Harry on the back and shake his hand energetically. At my side, Sally was smiling as she squeezed my arm.

'He's a special one, isn't he?'

I was somewhere between laughter and tears. My heart was swollen. He arrived back at my side and I couldn't speak, I was so full of love and pride. He was going to do such great things, we would move mountains together. Out of all the world, he had chosen me and he was mine.

JULY 24TH

HANNAH: *They've set a date for the trial.*
LIZZIE: *When?*
HANNAH: *Six weeks.*
LIZZIE: *How do you feel?*
HANNAH: *Relieved. Afraid.*
LIZZIE: *All that and more.*
HANNAH: *They say we're not allowed to speak on our own behalf.*
LIZZIE: *And no lawyers to speak for us either. What kind of justice is that?*
HANNAH: *We can call character witnesses.*
LIZZIE: *"I have known Lizzie Whitehead for many years and have found her to be an outspoken radical and atheist with a determination to overthrow the existing social order." That'd help, wouldn't it?*
HANNAH: *I wanted to have my say. I wanted to tell 'em what it was like to be famished, no matter how long you worked; to watch your family die one by one, for want of a rest and a decent meal and to see no way out, no end to it, until you die yourself.*
LIZZIE: *I know.*
HANNAH: *I know it was wrong, what we did, and that breaking the looms didn't help anybody to a better life, but it got us noticed, didn't it? It made 'em pay attention for once.*
LIZZIE: *Aye.*
HANNAH: *I've worked since I was seven years old at one thing or another and for most of that time I've been hungry, cold and tired to the bone.*
LIZZIE: *And angry.*
HANNAH: *That's what keeps me going.*

LIZZIE: *The fine men in that courtroom know what you've*
                suffered, lass. They know it well, and you telling 'em
                again wouldn't make an 'apeth of difference.
HANNAH: *It would to me.*

I was learning my lines in a quiet corner of the Hall, before everyone arrived for the meeting, when the swing doors flew open with a crash and Tom strode in, his arms full of boxes.

'Lend a hand, Charlie old girl.'

We borrow books from the Labour Party Library and this was a new shipment. I helped him load them onto a table.

'Thanks. Some jolly good titles this time.'

'No reading for me. Too busy.'

'Ah yes. Harry's masterpiece. Don't let me interrupt you further.'

'It's fine. It's nearly time for the meeting.'

Behind us, the doors crashed open again.

'The Fascists are out! They're on the Common.' Harry threw his bag of books and papers to the floor and dropped his jacket beside them. 'They're handing out copies of *The Blackshirt*. Come on. We'll play them at their own game.'

He grabbed a pile of our newspapers and ran out again. Tom and I exchanged a look, took an armful of *New Nations* and followed him. As we flew out of the door onto the street, we passed Sally going in.

'Fascists on the Common!' I gasped. 'Spread the word!'

They were behind a cluster of trees, a small group of men in black tunics and wide belts and a middle-aged man standing on a chair. It wasn't Mosley. Since the awful violence at the Olympia rally, support has waned for the BUF but apparently the great man still had bigger fish to fry than this small affair on Ealing Common. A few passers-by had stopped to listen to the speaker. He wasn't in uniform but wore a smart suit and tie. Well-spoken too. Perfectly respectable.

'Under Fascism, no foreigners shall enter this country to take your jobs. And those already here, who have abused the hospitality of our nation, shall be sent back where they belong.'

'That goes for the bloody Welsh, too,' shouted one of the Blackshirts at the front.

The Depression had brought people from the valleys, looking

for work in the city and they were blamed for driving down wages. There were 'Welsh Go Home' signs daubed on railway arches and 'English Only' in the windows of boarding houses.

'Don't blame your fellow workers,' shouted Harry as we reached the back of the group. 'Blame the greedy bosses.'

'Blame government cuts,' yelled Tom, waving a copy of the *New Nation*. 'Here, sir, read a decent newspaper, not that fascist rag.'

He and Harry waded through the crowd, offering our papers. The BUF men exchanged hostile looks and moved to intercept them. I watched anxiously, my heart beating hard in my chest. We were seriously outnumbered.

'The BUF puts Britons First,' cried the man on the box.

'Not if you're Jewish,' shouted a young woman a few feet from me. She smiled and nodded to the papers I was holding. 'Can I have one of those?'

Before I could pass it over, a bruiser of a man pushed his way to where we were standing and ripped it from my hand.

'Push off, Missy.'

He was very close to me, half-leering, half-threatening. He smelled of cigarettes. Under his thin moustache, his teeth were tobacco stained and his fingers were nicotine yellow. I backed away from his breath and tried very hard not to look as frightened as I felt.

'If you want a copy so badly, you only had to ask,' I said.

The woman laughed out loud and I felt elated for the briefest moment before he made a lunge at me and knocked me off my feet. I fell awkwardly and jarred my shoulder as he crushed the paper into a ball and cast it aside. That was when Harry appeared, like a whirlwind from nowhere, and pushed him away from me.

'Hands off!' he panted.

'I'm alright,' I said, scrambling to my feet. I didn't want him to think I couldn't handle the situation though, in truth, I was quaking in my boots.

He flashed me a grin full of love and pride that made me glow.

'See that?' he turned to the Blackshirt. 'That's a Socialist. Knock one down and two get up.'

'Oh yeah? Let's see how many get up from this.'

The blow was like a hammer. Harry staggered back and I cried out. The crowd parted as more Blackshirts pushed through. Harry got a few punches in before he fell but I saw a kick to his prone body as they closed around him. I screamed his name and ran at them but I couldn't break through. Then, like a miracle, Tom appeared, knocking them right and left and they scattered. I saw Harry get to all fours and struggle to his feet. He was holding his ribs but still in one piece and I was light-headed with relief. But not for long. As the Fascists regrouped and piled into Tom, he launched himself back into battle. Two against many, they were overwhelmed and fear gripped me like a vice. I threw myself at the jeering wall of black but I couldn't reach Harry, couldn't see him. My head was full of terrible visions of his beaten face and broken body. I heard myself shouting words that would make my mother faint with horror.

'Call your dogs off!' I screamed at the speaker, but he just stood watching and smirked at me.

Frantic, I ran to the chair he had abandoned, lifted it and brought it crashing down on the Blackshirt blocking my way. It broke on his back and I picked up a fractured leg and lashed out, catching the side of his head. I heard the crunch of wood on bone and my heart clenched in horror as he dropped to the ground and lay still at my feet. Looking up, I saw Harry staring at me over the prone body. I dropped the weapon and started to shake.

That was when Sally arrived with a dozen comrades from the League. Seeing them pelting across the grass, the enemy fell back and gathered around their leader. He gave them a sign and they dropped their hands, scowling, as we drew together in a breathless, watchful group. The man I had felled stirred and moaned. He wasn't dead. Thank God he wasn't dead. He was helped to his feet and stood unsteadily, blood in his hair and on the hand that cradled his head.

Harry put an arm around me. He had a bloody nose, a split lip and a bruise forming on his jaw. I realised he wasn't wearing his glasses.

'I always take them off when it gets rough,' he said. 'And not seeing what's bearing down on you is a bonus.'

He was trying to lighten the mood but it didn't work. I felt sick.

'Charlotte—'

I turned when I heard my name and my heart lurched in my chest. My father was standing on the path a few feet away. He was dressed for an evening out, white tie under his overcoat and a silk hat in his hands. I registered his shock and disapproval and then I saw how much he had aged. Six months to make him an old man.

'I went to the school and they told me you were here.'

I felt the blood rush to my cheeks. How much had he seen? The Blackshirts were leaving. They marched away, saluting and chanting slogans. I looked at my father. Couldn't he see what they were? That someone had to take a stand against them? But it seemed that the condemnation in his face was all for me.

'What are you thinking, Charlotte? Have you lost all self-respect?'

Harry squeezed my hand and it brought me to life.

'This is my father,' I said. 'Father, this is Harry.'

'Pleased to meet you, sir.'

He held out a hand but it wasn't taken. Father stood like a statue, staring at Harry's dusty clothes and battered face. Tom and the others moved away, anxious to spare my feelings. I was trying not to cry. This was my father and I loved him. I was ashamed of him and angry with him, but I loved him and seeing the weariness in his familiar face, the price of our estrangement, twisted my heart. I took a step towards him but he backed away. His face crumpled then re-formed into anger and disgust. He was horrified by me.

'This ends here,' he said. 'I've come to take you home.'

I stared at him in disbelief. How could he think that was possible?

'You won't even try to understand, will you?'

'A public brawl.' He looked towards the broken chair, still in pieces on the grass. 'You might have seriously injured that man. He could have you arrested.'

'The Fascists give as good as they get,' said Harry. 'More, actually.'

Father rounded on him with a horrible mixture of anger and contempt.

'She's eighteen years old. Have you no sense of responsibility?

You're a bunch of hooligans!'

'These are my comrades,' I said. 'I'm proud to stand with them.'

'You choose them over your family?'

'I don't want to choose. You're forcing me to do it.'

'You're breaking your mother's heart.'

I cried then, faced with the pain I knew I was causing. But anger flared in me too. I let go of Harry's hand and stood strong, facing my father's condemnation with a determination that surprised me.

'It doesn't have to be like this,' I told him, through tears. 'You can accept me. You don't have to approve. You just have to let it be.'

'Nonsense!'

'If you give me an ultimatum, I won't choose home.'

'The choice isn't yours to make. You're under age.'

'If you force me back, I'll run away. If you send me away, I'll come back here. This is where I belong now.'

'I'll cut you off without a penny.'

'That's up to you.'

We were eye to eye and finally I saw the realisation take hold of him, that there was nothing he could do to change my mind. He seemed to deflate, to look smaller, and I knew it was over. The silk hat trembled in his hands and he tightened his grip on it.

'So be it.'

I wanted to run to him, kiss his cheek, be held to his chest and feel safe from all danger. I wanted to be his little girl again. But it was too late for that. As he walked away, I reached for Harry's hand.

'Are you alright?' he asked. 'Do you want to go after him?'

'No.'

'Are you sure? It's your father.'

I shook my head and he passed me his handkerchief to dry my tears. There was blood on it from his nose and lip, a few deep red spots, like badges of honour.

'No one calls me Charlotte,' I called out.

'What?' my father turned back.

'It's Charlie,' I said to him. 'I'm Charlie now.'

2003

The longest minute of my life. My urine, the waste product of my body, passing judgement, holding sway for sixty eternal seconds. After weeks waiting for blood, more waiting, crouched silent in the locked bathroom in the empty house. The grandfather clock in the hall booming the half hour and suddenly all the clocks, in every room, audible, every dragging second. Sitting on the closed toilet seat watching the plastic strip, watching it change colour, watching the betrayal of my body. One minute to confirm I'm no longer in charge, no longer at liberty. Confinement—an old term suddenly takes on new meaning.

'I don't know what to do.'

'It was unplanned then?'

'Completely.'

'You don't have other children?'

'No. I never made a conscious decision not to have them. It's just that there were always other priorities. I suppose I didn't want them enough.'

'Nor me.'

'But do you regret it now?'

Charlie shakes her head. There is no doubt in her eyes when she replies.

'Sometimes I regret that I missed a little piece of immortality. But that's all.'

The light is fading as the sun dips out of sight.

'I'm not sure if this is a world I want to bring a child into.'

'Then you aren't seeing it clearly. The world is full of wonders.'

'I've lost sight of that.'

There is a breeze coming in from the sea and Charlie pulls her cardigans around her, crossing her arms to hold them wrapped around her body.

'Many years ago, when I was sad and afraid, a dear comrade told me to put one foot in front of the other till the darkness lifted. It was advice she learned from the love of her life, passed down a family for generations, then to me. Now I pass it on to you. Just keep going, my dear. Persist. That's the wisest counsel I can give you.'

*

It is the end of the night in the taverna and they are the last to leave. The waiters are sitting at a table outside, smoking and drinking retsina. No hurry says Ioseph, the owner. He and Charlie are old friends. He calls her Madame West and gives them dessert and coffee on the house.

'How did you come to live here?' asks Margaret.

'It was a happy accident. I was living in Chelsea with an artist—'

'Why doesn't that surprise me?'

Charlie laughs.

'I'll take that as a compliment. It was Nigel who wanted to move abroad. Somewhere south, for the light. Dear Nigel. He was a lovely man. Mad as a hatter but a heart of gold. Anyway, my parents were long gone, and I finally sold the family home, so there was nothing holding me in England. We came here on a whim and on the first day I saw this house was for sale. I fell in love with it and with the island and that was that.'

'Have you never been back?'

'To visit. But this is home.' She helps herself to more honey-soaked baklava. 'Your turn now. Tell me about Downing Street. Was there nothing good about it?'

'Working for Alastair Campbell? It was a laugh a minute.'

'Nothing that makes you proud?'

'Nothing that cancels out this war.'

Charlie licks her sticky fingers.

'The Minimum Wage? The Human Rights Act?'

'Of course. And a lot more. We're re-building the NHS after the Tories nearly ended it. And education, and child benefit— lots of stuff. I know that, but—'

'The war.'

'Not just that. We could do so much more, we could finally shift the balance of power, change the system. Imagine that? But the will isn't there. That's not what New Labour is about. Eighteen

124

years we waited for a Labour government and when we got one with the power to move mountains, we pissed it up the wall. Sorry.'

'No apology necessary.'

A girl on a Vespa pulls up by the table of waiters and one of them drains his glass and climbs on behind her. As they drive away he waves back with his free hand, the other on her waist. She is a beauty. His friends exchange knowing looks and smiles. The sound of the engine fades into the distance and Charlie leans forward.

'Do you stop fighting for right because wrong is winning?' She laughs. 'I know. Big question. I can be rather grand, my dear. Bear with me.'

'I don't mind. I'm rather preoccupied with big questions at the moment.'

'That's alright then. So, what's the answer?'

'How do you touch them? A million people marched through London and for what? Nothing.'

'It's never for nothing.'

'Tell that to Iraq.'

'You've lost your way.'

'I'm tired.'

'But you were full of fight and passion once.'

Margaret is drawing lines on the tablecloth with her fork.

'I can't remember.'

'Yes, you can.'

'Charlie—'

'When? Tell me.'

She sent the police on horseback, charging into the crowd, beating them with batons.

'Twenty years ago.' She looks up. 'The Miners' Strike.'

'Ah. Thatcher. That'll do it.'

Margaret puts down the fork and smooths out the scored white linen with her fingers.

'My dad's family all worked down the pit, for generations. He was the first not to spend his life underground. But when the strike was lost, on the day they marched back to work, he cried. I found him sitting in front of the television news, in tears. The only other time I'd ever seen him cry was at my mum's funeral—and there he was.'

125

The view through the window blurs. Her throat aches. There is a burst of laughter from the waiters outside. The boss has joined them and is passing around a bottle of Metaxa. Inside, in the quiet of the empty restaurant, Charlie reaches out and takes Margaret's hand.

'Go on.'

'I wrote a piece about the strike, about the communities being thrown on the waste heap, and my dad was so proud when he read it. He said if he'd known about Thatcher when I was born he'd never have called me Margaret! But that it didn't matter now, that I'd reclaimed my name for the good side.'

'That's a fine memory.'

'It was a good feeling.'

'You'll get it back, my dear.'

'I wish I could believe that.'

'One foot in front of the other.'

Seeing Charlie's face, full of affection, Margaret realises how grateful she is for this unsought friendship and its sudden intimacy.

'I'm glad we met, Charlie.'

'So am I, my dear.'

The band around her chest loosens a notch for the first time in months.

'What happened to Nigel?'

'Oh, he moved on, bless him. We keep in touch.' There is one square of baklava left on the plate. Charlie offers it to Margaret and when she shakes her head, takes it herself, laughing as she chews. 'The last I heard he was in Morocco. Apparently, the light there is inspirational.'

*

I know there are women who long for this everyday miracle, new life from old, who won't be satisfied with anything but motherhood. I'm not made that way. If this thing hadn't happened, I would have gone on oblivious. Now the choice is everything. I'm forty years old. It's likely to be my last chance, if I want a chance. The child might have problems. Or it might be perfectly formed and still devastate my life. Or it might be my salvation. And that last, seductive idea must be the worst, false hope of a reason ever for having a baby.

*

'Margaret!'

Charlie hails her from a table at a seafront bar. She is sitting with a man and woman who look to be in their forties, both sleek, tanned and prosperous.

'Margaret — meet James and Sarah, my part-time neighbours.'

'You have a house here?' she asks.

'The one with the blue shutters.'

'It's lovely.'

'Yes, it is,' Sarah says. 'Sadly we don't spend enough time in it.'

'Work.' James shrugs. 'You know how it is.'

'Sarah and James run a PR company.' Charlie's eyes twinkle at her across the table.

Of course they do.

'Snowed under,' Sarah shakes her head.

'The price of success,' James is a study in mock diffidence.

She is mentally rehearsing excuses for a swift departure, but Charlie gets in first, with a mischievous smile.

'Margaret is a journalist. She worked in the Downing Street Press Office.'

That gets their attention. As both pairs of eyes fix on her with new interest, she moves to shut the conversation down.

'I was just one of many in the background. And I left months ago.'

'Did Campbell have a tantrum and fire you?' James laughs.

'I didn't give him the chance.'

'He's a blunt instrument, isn't he?' Sarah smiles. 'But he gets the job done.'

'The job?'

James runs a manicured hand through his abundant greying hair.

'They've turned the Labour Party around, that's for sure. Dragged it kicking and screaming into the 21st century.'

Charlie is sipping her wine and staring out to sea. Her face is impassive.

Nice move. I'll get you for this.

'Blair is a player,' says Sarah. 'He realises the value of a good suit and a seat at Murdoch's table.'

James nods his assent.

'He's positioned Labour where it needs to be.'

Knowing she shouldn't rise to it, feeling the old frustration and a new weariness, Margaret still can't help herself.

'Just a bit nicer than the Tories.'

They both stare at her.

'Not a fan?' asks James.

I've met so many of you, so many Jameses and Sarahs, so many decent people with a good heart and a social conscience, talking about aspiration and social mobility and trickle-down prosperity. Not even aware how resistant they are to actual, lasting change and anyone who suggests attempting it.

'Margaret is an idealist,' Charlie says brightly.

'Ideals are useless without power.' Sarah's tone is a shade away from patronising.

'And power is pointless without ideals.'

James shrugs his shoulders and smiles knowingly.

'And there we have it. Principles or pragmatism? Labour's great dilemma.'

They walk back to the house together, their arms linked, the soft wool of Charlie's cardigan brushing Margaret's bare skin, a faint scent of Chanel and talcum powder, a veined old hand clasping her wrist as they walk slowly down the shore.

'Maybe they're right,' Margaret says. 'Maybe people don't want a Welfare State if they have to pay for it. Maybe they mistrust immigrants, hate the gays and love the Queen. Maybe the only way to get elected is to be no threat to Rupert Murdoch.'

'And maybe we'd vote for fairness if we were ever offered it. Who knows till we try.'

'James and Sarah think they know.'

Charlie laughs. 'Your face was a picture!'

'You're a wicked woman.'

'You say you've lost your fight. That isn't what I saw, my dear.'

'You set me up.'

'I did. I admit it.'

Margaret shakes her head.

'Getting angry is easy. Believing you can do anything about what makes you angry—that's a whole different thing.'

They are passing a bench by the harbour wall. Charlie squeezes Margaret's arm.

'Let's have a seat.'

They sit looking out to sea, with the breeze on their faces. For a while, they are silent, listening to the gulls overhead and the incoming tide slapping the rocks of the breakwater. Then Charlie pulls her cardigans around her and turns with a smile.

'Do you think the first Trade Unionists, being blacklisted, imprisoned and transported, never gave way to doubt? What about the Chartists and the Suffragettes, fighting for centuries to get the vote? Or the ANC in South Africa, under apartheid? I'll bet many of them despaired during the struggle. Who wouldn't?'

Margaret reaches up to push her windblown hair from her face, clasping her hands at her hairline to shade her eyes from the sun.

'I hear what you're saying. I just don't know how to carry on.'

'One foot in front of the other?' Charlie takes both Margaret's hands in hers and looks into her face. 'Can you do that?'

'It sounds so easy.'

'And yet it can be so hard.'

Margaret lets out her breath with a sigh and returns Charlie's smile with a weak one of her own.

'I'm not as strong as you.'

'Nonsense.'

'It's true.'

Charlie shakes her head.

'I have my weaknesses, believe me.'

'Well, I think you're remarkable.'

'No.'

With a sudden unease between them, Charlie lets go of Margaret's hands and pushes herself upright.

'Shall we go?'

'If you like.'

'It's a little chilly.'

Margaret stands and, as they fall into step together towards Charlie's house, she asks, 'Is something wrong? What did I say?'

'Nothing. It's nothing.'

'It doesn't feel like nothing.'

Charlie doesn't reply immediately. As they reach the terrace, she seems to shake herself.

'I'm sorry. I let the past in for a while. There are things I'm not proud of.'

'We can all say that.'

'Don't put me on a pedestal.'

'Why not? We all need heroes.'

'And we must choose our heroes wisely.'

They have stopped walking. Charlie is very still, her thoughts turned inward, but Margaret can't let it go. Against all her normal instincts, she keeps pushing against Charlie's resistance.

'What are you not telling me?'

'I'm not who you think I am. I've led a pampered life. I was only tested once, and I failed. The rest costs me nothing.'

'I don't understand.'

'There's no reason why you should.' At last, Charlie smiles her old smile, and with relief, Margaret feels the tension between them dissolve. 'It's alright, my dear.'

'I'm sorry if I upset you.'

'You didn't.'

'You look tired.'

'Yes. It's past time for my nap. We'll talk tomorrow.'

'You don't have to tell me anything.'

'I want to.'

'Alright then.'

'Come to lunch tomorrow and I'll tell you about Harry.'

*

He is wearing the clothes he left in, the corduroy trousers, the dark green sweater, the short tweed jacket and his beloved cap. Charlie has no idea where they are. A timeless, formless no-man's land, at once familiar and foreign. She is eighty-five and Harry is still twenty. It doesn't matter.

'Tom told me how you died,' she says. 'I made him tell me everything.'

'You needed to know.'

'I needed to know.' Every tiny detail. To fill the emptiness with something, anything, even agony. 'You were holding a bridge over the Jarama River.'

'We were outnumbered about ten to one. There was no real cover and we were crouched behind olive trees for two days with the rifles almost too hot to hold because we'd been firing constantly.'

'Then you were hit.' She had played that moment over and over in her head. The bullet. The blood. His body reeling back. A cry. 'There were no stretchers, so Tom volunteered to be yours.'

'They laid me on top of him—'

'And carried the two of you away from the action.'

'I bled all over him. I saw him later, trying to wash his shirt in an irrigation channel and I remember thinking, that's my blood watering the fields of Spain.'

He is so young.

'Were you afraid?'

'Every day.'

Charlie is submerged in loss, sucked under and drowning in the waste of it.

'We could have had such a life together.'

'I know.'

'Such a life.'

*

The rain wakes her at four in the morning, lashing the roof and veranda doors, a wild, noisy downpour. The first rain she has seen here, Margaret watches it with new eyes, feels its strangeness, like a child's first sight of snow. No English drizzle but strong needles of water, driven by the wind—sudden swirling activity slashing the still night, rattling windows and pitting the surface of the pewter sea.

With sleep banished, she turns on the television. She has it set to CNN with the volume off. The images flicker in the dark room. Massive silhouettes of armoured tanks against the eerie strangeness of night-vision green. Helicopters churning sand and American flags strobing in the heat haze. Soldiers crouching and running through a jagged rubble of smashed buildings. The rope lights of a city slashed by the sheet lightning of incoming shells. Bursts of white smoke and billows of yellow in the night sky. Blurred satellite images of compounds in colourless deserts, white lines on targets exploding in black and grey. Children in hospital beds, traumatised into wide-eyed silence. Bloodied bodies on stretchers, corpses in the dust. Mourners keening over body bags.

In her mind's eye, she sees the sea of people marching through London on a chilly February day, children on parents' shoulders, banners and placards, a mass of protesters filling the streets, an outpouring of anger and despair. She hears the chanting and singing, the speeches in Hyde Park, the warnings ringing from the platform to echo through history.

'This will set off a spiral of conflict, of hate, of desperation, that will fuel the wars, the terrorism and the misery of future generations.'

All those faces, all those desperate pleas to be heard. All for nothing. The decision had been made long before the march for peace. No-one was listening. There was no pulling back from this planned and manufactured war.

As dawn breaks and the room slowly lightens, she feels guilt finally give way to anger and, somewhere beneath it, the first, faint stirrings of determination. She presses the remote and the pictures on the TV screen disappear.

Outside, the clouds are dispersing in the last gusts of wind and stillness is reasserting itself, settling warm and quiet over land and sea. Somewhere in the distance, a church bell is tolling, calling the faithful. The believers.

There will be candles and incense, golden icons flickering in the light, faces thrown in shadow, there will be music and prayer.

When I was fifteen, a boy I knew discovered God one night, a sensible, intelligent boy who met me the next day with a steady radiance in his face and a determination that I should share his certainty. It made an impression on me. In my bed, in the dark, I closed my eyes and prayed. I felt the night all around me. I felt nature. I felt humanity. I didn't feel God.

My friend gave up. He gave me up too. A few years ago, by chance, I saw him again. He still has that unshakeable faith and I am filled with incomprehension at a life built on something so far removed from my reality.

Without God, we must find different answers to the universal questions, different truths, a new creed to live by.

*

'He was my first and best love,' says Charlie.

'What happened?'

'He was killed in Spain, fighting the Fascists.'

She says it lightly but, for a second, her eyes darken and Margaret knows this is old pain that can still flare fresh and raw more than half a century after it was born.

'I'm so sorry.'

They are in Charlie's bright dining room. A white vase holds a mass of cerise bougainvillea. A large canvas on the wall is vivid with blue sea and sky. The sunlight is streaming in through the open windows. The voile curtain across the French doors is billowing softly in the light breeze from the terrace.

Charlie opens the table drawer and takes out a faded photograph.

'Here he is.'

No more than a boy really. Tall and slim. Dark hair and round glasses.

'The Fascists were marching across Europe. The International Brigade fought for a better world when no-one else would. It was what he believed and what I thought I believed. Until I had to live it.' She touches the black and white face staring up at them through time. 'We talked endlessly about fighting the good fight but when the time came I couldn't do it. I begged him not to go.'

'That's the test you failed?'

'I told him he was putting the cause above me. I told him I would never forgive him for going. They were the last words I ever said to him.'

'How old were you?'

'Eighteen.'

'Little more than a child.'

There is defiance in Charlie's face. She dismisses Margaret's justification with an impatient shake of the head.

'I'm a fraud. I'd see swastikas flying from every rooftop in Europe if we could just have our time together, our precious time—if he could just not be dead. That's the wish of my secret heart. Even now.'

Margaret feels a tide of affection and, at the same time, a sense of something more, of the understanding that must come before acceptance. She feels a shift in her heart and mind. A new stability.

'Whatever you've wished,' she says, 'it isn't how you've lived.'

'I can't forgive him for dying.'

'It's yourself you can't forgive.' Margaret smiles wryly. 'Trust me on that.'

Charlie's eyes are bright with tears, but she laughs as they fall, wiping her face with her cardigan sleeve.

'What a pair we are!'

'You've made a difference,' Margaret says. 'If you want to hold yourself to an impossible standard I can't stop you, but you won't change my opinion of you. You've made a difference to me.'

'Thank you, my dear.'

Carrying the torch. Just carrying on. When your head and heart are screaming that you can't.

'Do you think we'll ever see the world we wish for?'

A few vivid pink petals have fallen from the flowers onto the table and Charlie sweeps them together with a finger before she speaks.

'At the moment, there's no one in power saying what we want to hear, but that could change.' She raises her eyes, dry now, but still fierce with purpose. 'It could change in a heartbeat. History has taught us that.'

'And till then?'

'Decide what you believe in and fight for it. Draw the line and stand on it firmly—like Harry did. Like you did.'

'Me?'

'You resigned. On principle.'

'Eventually.'

'Small acts, my dear. Ripples in the stream that eventually wear away the stone. Do your best. What more can any of us do?'

Charlie gets up and throws the petals out of the window. The breeze catches them and they dance in the air briefly, like pink snowflakes. She picks up Harry's photograph and props it against the vase.

'He has no grave. They were buried where they fell, somewhere in the Jarama Valley. I've never been there but I want to see it now. It's time.' She turns to Margaret. 'I have a favour to ask, my dear. Will you come to Spain with me?'

1937

WEDNESDAY was the King's coronation. Eight horses pulled a gold coach to Westminster Abbey. A man in a priceless crown, bishops in gilded robes, lords in scarlet and ermine, ladies in coronets and jewels. Glittering like bloated queen bees whilst the workers lined the streets and cheered, trained to come when called, like dogs to the whistle.

Harry thought it could be different. Our boy. Dead in a Spanish field and our hearts buried with him. Dead for nowt. Wasted. Like his father before him. Duped and murdered and nothing changes. Nothing ever changes.

He would have been twenty-one today. When I came down this morning, Rose was at the kitchen table, weeping. She was with me when he was born, she mothered him all his life, he was as much hers as he was mine. I took her in my arms and she shook with sobs, her head under my chin, her tears soaking my dress. I stroked her hair, staring over her to the chair where he always sat, longing to see him there, blood and bone aching for the sight of him. No tears though. I shed rivers in the beginning, but they dried up. I'm hard as rock now, brittle as glass.

Rose cried herself out and went still and quiet. The only sound was the clock ticking on the mantlepiece. There was a spider's web on the outside of the window, jewelled with raindrops, sparkling as the sun caught it. I tried to think of words for how I felt. Hollowed out. Weighted down. None of them got anywhere near. Harry would know how to describe it. He was always full to the brim with words. All gone now. All dust.

'I'll make some tea.' Rose looked up into my face. Her eyes were swollen, her skin streaked and blotchy with grief. She went on tip-toe and kissed me softly, her tears wet on my dry lips. 'Sit by the stove,' she said. 'You're cold.'

I watched her fill the kettle, warm the pot and set out the cups, fetch the milk from the larder, spoon the leaves. The tea ritual.

There was something comforting in the routine, something constant, something from before. From now on everything will be measured as before and after. Nothing changes but nothing will be the same.

Charlie came in, still in her dressing gown. Pale face, dark circles under her eyes and her hair needed washing. Every movement seemed an effort. Poor little lass. She's nineteen and her youth has been wiped away by sorrow. She sat at the table and accepted a cup of tea, without speaking. Putting out a hand, she touched the arm of Harry's chair then flinched away as if it had burnt her. Pain swelled in me like a scream.

'I've sorted cover today,' Rose said. 'The girls are going on a field trip to the Natural History Museum. We can have some time to ourselves.'

'That was kind.' Charlie tucked a greasy strand of hair behind her ear.

I remembered the first time she came here, not much more than a year ago. Sitting at this table, on her birthday, bright-eyed and full of life, brimming over with possibilities.

'I'm sorry, Charlie,' I said. 'I'm sorry I didn't help you. When you tried to make him stay.'

We had all been in this kitchen, at this same table, when he told us he was going to fight in Spain. He and Tom had signed up, he said. They had joined the International Brigade and they were going to fight the Fascists. He stood looking at us, his eyes moving from face to face, his hair tusselled and untidy as always, a smudge of printer's ink on his cheek, his eyes bright behind his wire glasses. In the shocked quiet that followed his announcement, he took them off and polished them with the end of the tablecloth, to cover his nervousness. He looked strangely vulnerable without them and heart-achingly young. My boy. My lost boy.

It was Charlie who had broken the silence. She was shaking her head, her eyes bewildered.

'What about our work here? What about the people who need you here?'

'Spain needs me more.'

'What about me? I need you. What about me?'

He flashed me a look, but I couldn't help him. Rose and me

136

were staring at each other's frightened faces, remembering our war and the dead and broken bodies it delivered, day after bloody day.

'Try to understand, love.'

'I'm not your love. You don't love me. You don't care about me at all.'

'You know that isn't true.'

'I don't.' Charlie got to her feet, tears streaming and eyes flashing. 'You didn't even tell me before you signed your life away. What I think doesn't matter. That's clear enough.'

I could see how hard it was for him to hurt her so badly, but I knew him and I saw that nothing was going to change his mind. Charlie was right. It didn't matter what any of us thought.

'I have to go. I just have to.'

He reached out to take her arm but she tore herself away from him.

'Go then. Go and play soldiers.'

She stormed out and the door crashed to a close behind her. For a second, it looked like he was going to run after her, but he checked himself. He put a hand to the chair back, as if for support, and looked up at Rose and me. My heart contracted. It was like he was a small boy again, looking for me to make it better.

'She'll never forgive me, Mum.'

'She's frightened.'

'I know. That's what I can't stand.' He took a step towards me. 'Do you think I'm wrong?'

That was the moment. I keep going back to it, in my head. Over and over. Twisting the knife in the wound. That was my chance and I threw it away. I should have told him, yes, he was wrong. I should have fought his certainty with every fibre of me, but instead I told him that he had to do what he thought was right. Stupid. Unforgivable. Because the terrible truth is that, under the fear, part of me was proud of him, proud of the cause.

Harry believed in justice because I taught him to believe. I fed him full of hope and passion and it killed him. Every word from me was a bullet in the gun that ended him. I should have known that wrong would win, like it always does, that all the courage and sacrifice was just a waste of life. I should have coaxed and blamed, shouted and cried, like Charlie did. I should have kept him here. I'm his mother. I should have saved him.

Rose took my hand in one of hers and reached out for Charlie's with the other. We sat joined together as a rain shower pattered the window and the spider's web wafted and settled again beside the glass.

That day last year, Charlie's birthday, was when we got our first look at Harry's play, the song about workers being sacrificed to progress. So many times, over the years, me and Rose would listen to scenes from his latest epic, act them out with him, being pirates, explorers, detectives, finding the treasure, catching the culprit. He grew up and the plays grew with him, till *One Foot in Front of the Other*. The play he was born to write. His last. His epitaph. The League were rehearsing it when he left for Spain and by the time they took it on the arranged trip up north, he was deep in the fighting. Charlie said it helped her feel close to him, playing his flesh and blood, saying his words. One foot in front of the other. Lizzie's lesson. It isn't working this time.

One of my classes with the girls is to take them through the day's newspapers. We look at what's happening, how it's being presented. We talk about whether newspapers just report the news or whether they create it, and what their motives might be. Question everything, I tell them. Make your own mind up. Have an opinion.

Just now it's hard to find anything but the coronation on page after page. Pictures of the royals posed on the palace balcony, vast crowds in The Mall. The young princesses, like dolls in crowns, waving and smiling to order. What are they thinking up there? What a strange psychological experiment their lives are, trained from birth to uphold the big lie.

Not long ago I would have jumped at the chance of talking to the girls about monarchy and class and inherited privilege. It's always been meat and drink to me. But, looking into their faces now, I struggle. I feel the weight of their expectations and I've got nothing to give them. I've always believed that what we say and do, how we live, makes a difference, that we're all part of a tide that will wash away the world's injustice, inch by inch. I don't believe that any more.

'What are we doing here?' I asked Rose as she curled into me last night. I'd left a chink between the curtains when I drew them and there was a pale stripe of moonlight across the bed, just catching the hand she laid on my arm. 'I don't know what we're doing anymore.'

She raised her head and looked down at mine on the pillow. Her face was in shadow, but I knew what her expression would be, full of love and sympathy, a worried wrinkle between her eyes. Her hair was loose about her shoulders and it brushed my cheek as she bent and kissed my forehead.

'We're changing lives, my love. We're following the plan.' She ran her fingers along my eyebrows, easing the tension. 'We're passing it on.'

'Do you remember asking me, back on Lemnos, if I ever lose heart?'

'Ten times a day, you said.'

'I didn't know what it meant then. I had no idea.'

Her face was very close to mine. I could feel her breath, warm on my skin.

'You heart isn't lost,' she said. 'It's broken.'

The moon went behind a cloud and the room dimmed. She held me, rocked me, as I wailed like a wounded animal, great dry sobs ripping and tearing. How much did he suffer? How afraid was he? Did he call for me, like the lads from Gallipoli called for their mothers as the darkness came for them? I wasn't there. I didn't make it better. I can never make it better.

Across the table, Charlie surfaced from her thoughts, freed her hand and stood up.

'I'll be in my room if you need me.'

'Are you going to the League meeting tonight?' Rose asked.

'Probably not.'

'It might do you good to get out, see some friends.'

'It's too hard.'

We watched her walk heavily to the door and go out.

'Just when she seemed to be rallying a little,' said Rose.

'We're all back at square one today.'

'I know.' She turned my hand over and kissed my palm. 'I love you.'

'And I love you.'

'We won't let this part us, will we?'

There was real fear in her eyes. I pulled her into me and held her tight.

*

The rain had cleared away and there were patches of pale blue sky appearing between the clouds. I was at the sink washing our few breakfast pots, watching the spider climbing the single thread it had spun between its web and the pale branches of a hibiscus bush beside the window. For a while it stopped, hanging in the air, motionless, and I stood with my hands in the soapy water, waiting for it to move again, waiting for a sign that life goes on. I don't know how long I was there but when the doorbell rang I woke to the fact that the water was cold and the plates were still dirty. I grabbed a tea towel to wipe my hands and went through to the hall, but Rose had beaten me to it and opened the door.

The woman on the step had a faded hat pinned tight to her greying hair. Her old coat was sponged and brushed, her scuffed shoes polished. She had put on her best to come here.

'I'm Annie's mother.'

'Yes,' Rose said. 'I know who you are, Mrs Parker. Come in, please.'

We led her into what we call the Visitors' Room, where the girls can entertain their guests. Rose gestured towards a chair, but Mrs Parker shook her head.

'I can't stay.' Her voice was strained. She looked weary. 'I've come to tell you Annie has to leave. We need her at home.'

Rose gave me a quick, startled glance before she took a step forward, her face full of concern.

'Sit down, please. Tell us what's happened.'

Mrs Parker capitulated and perched on the edge of a chair, stiff-backed and defensive.

'Her dad lost his job last month. There's no work.' She had her hands on her lap, rough, red hands clasped so tight that her knuckles were white against the dark fabric of her coat. 'We've sold everything we had. The Means Test Inspector docked the unemployment pay because we had too many chairs and blankets. Well, they're gone now. There's nothing left to sell.'

'I'm so sorry,' Rose said.

Mrs Parker raised her eyes, desperate defiance in her face.

'Her little brothers aren't old enough to work yet. One of the big houses I clean for needs a girl to help in the kitchen and says they'll take Annie.'

I was standing by the door, leaving Rose to deal with the situation. It was our routine that she was the meet and greeter. She was better at social pleasantries than me, her upbringing had taught her all that. But, as the story unfolded, I couldn't help myself, I moved in and sat down next to Rose.

'Mrs Parker—'

'I don't want her to leave here but there's nothing else to do.' She was a tall woman, but she seemed to shrink in her seat. Her face set hard and her eyes deadened. 'We need the money. We'll starve without it.'

'What will she earn?' I asked.

She looked straight at me for the first time and I held her gaze. I knew this woman, I understood her life in a way that Rose, with the best will in the world, never could. I'm safe now and so bloody lucky, but where I grew up, everybody was one pay packet away from desperation. It leaves its mark and I think she saw it in my face.

'The kitchen job. What will it pay?'

'Twenty-three shillings a week.'

'I'll give you that to let Annie stay.'

She didn't move, she just stared at me. The blood rushed into her face and drained away. Mistrust gave way to relief then anger in her eyes. I could read her thoughts. An unimagined answer, a way out, and then the realisation that her family could live or die for a sum of money I can afford to give away. That's the rotten world we live in.

Rose sat forward.

'Let us help Annie. Please.'

'Why would you?' asked Mrs Parker through white lips.

'She's a very special girl. A true genius. If she gets the education she deserves, her future is unbounded. Who knows what she could achieve?'

'It's charity.'

'Does that matter?'

'You're already housing her, feeding her, educating her.'

'That's what we do for all the girls.'

She looked past us to the big bay window with its stained-glass panels across the top and from there to the drapes, the rugs and the gilt mirror over the marble fireplace and I knew what she was thinking.

I first found Annie doing mental arithmetic tricks for a cinema

141

queue in the rain, shivering whilst she added and subtracted and multiplied for pennies. I took her home to tell her parents about the school. A family of six living in two damp rooms with peeling wallpaper and mould growing on the ceiling. Dark corridors and stairs led to a communal toilet and a shared water tap in a stinking alleyway. That's where this bleak-faced woman came from today, to sit in our warm, comfortable Visitors' Room, to get a little taste of a life she'll never know. I wanted to apologise, to ask forgiveness, but what good would that do? It would only ease me, not her.

'We can't take your money. It's not right.'

'For Annie.'

The pain in her eyes deepened.

'We could never pay you back.'

'It doesn't matter.'

'Maybe not to you.' She stood up, brushing back a stray hair from her brow. Her coat sleeve was darned at the elbow and fraying out at the cuff. Her face was pale and closed.

'Will you fetch her, please? I'm taking her home.'

'She isn't here,' Rose said. 'The girls are on an outing today.'

'Till when?'

'About six.'

Mrs Parker shook her head. 'I can't wait till then. I'm due at work.'

They stood facing each other awkwardly. Rose gave me an anxious look and I stepped forward.

'Let her stay here tonight. Say her goodbyes. I'll bring her to you tomorrow.'

She hesitated then nodded briefly and moved to the door. The three of us walked across the hall in silence, our steps echoing in the house strangely empty of running girls and calling voices. On the step, Mrs Parker paused and looked back at us.

'Thank you. For trying to help her.' There were tears in her eyes as she turned and walked away.

Rose closed the door and took a deep breath.

'We can't let this happen.'

'There's thousands of clever kids scrubbing floors and digging coal,' I said. 'What's one more?'

I didn't mean it and she knew I didn't. She reached for my hand.

142

'But Annie is our clever kid.'

'Aye. She is.'

'What are we going to do?'

'I don't know yet.' I saw a smile in her eyes. 'What?'

'Yet. It's a good word.'

The sun, through the glass over the door, was lighting up her hair, a few strands of silver glistening among the gold. Over twenty years since we fell in love amongst the blood and the bedpans. I was convinced I was the strong one then, but I was wrong. She stands firm in every storm. Her roots run deep. She's earthed, and I'd be lost in the whirlwind without her.

'What are you thinking?' she asked.

'Do you never wish you were squandering your money away in the south of France?'

'Never.'

'Do you wonder what your life might have been if we'd never met?'

'Empty.'

'I don't know who I am anymore.'

She cupped my hand in both of hers.

'I know you. That will have to be enough for now.'

'I didn't finish the washing up.'

'We'll do it now.'

We were nearly at the kitchen door when she stopped in her tracks and turned to me with a new thought bright in her eyes.

'What?'

'He could earn the money. Mr Parker. He could be our caretaker.'

'Do we need a caretaker?'

'Does it matter?' We stood there, smiling at each other. 'I bet Agnes would welcome more help with the housekeeping too, if Mrs Parker was interested.'

I had an idea. It hurt to think it, to say it, but I took a deep breath.

'The Lodge is empty now.' It was his. But he doesn't need it any more. 'We could get them out of that slum.'

Rose's eyes sparkled.

'Will they do it, do you think?'

'It's not charity.'

'A fair week's pay for a fair week's work.'

'I'll talk to them in the morning.'

'Let's go now.' She grabbed my arm. 'We might be able to catch her up.'

Life is cruel and unfair. Nothing we do changes that. I don't believe a better world is coming. I don't believe that justice will overcome greed. But I believe in kindness. I've seen what it can do. So many awful wrongs but we can right a small one today, at least.

'Get your coat,' I said. 'Let's get it settled.'

*

THE COURTROOM IN LANCASTER CASTLE

JUDGE: *Eliza Whitehead and Hannah Marsden—you are charged that on the 24th day of April 1826 you did participate in numerous acts of violence against textile mills in the County of Lancashire. After hearing the evidence against you, the gentlemen of the jury have found you guilty and it is now my solemn duty to pass sentence upon you.*

HANNAH: *Your Honour—*

JUDGE: *You know that you are not allowed to speak.*

LIZZIE: *We know it alright. There's no place for the truth in these proceedings.*

JUDGE: *Rioting is a sin against society by violating security of property, and a sin against God and the King by disobeying the King's God-given law.*

HANNAH: *People were starving!*

JUDGE: *However pitiable your situation, you should not have taken the remedy into your own hands. Poverty is a natural part of life, to be alleviated, not by violent insurrection but by charity. The condition of security and social order is obedience to the law and it is necessary you be taught that you must never again attempt to remedy your distress by acts of violence. You will be transported upon the seas to such as His Majesty shall think fit to direct and appoint, for the term of seven years.*

HANNAH: *Your Honour, I have a child—*

JUDGE: *It is unfortunate you did not think of that before participating in these disgraceful events. I hope this*

144

	period of exile will serve as a lesson that no happiness can result from a life of turbulence and riot.
LIZZIE:	*Exile will be a blessing to us. Haven't we been exiles in our own land for years? This isn't a punishment, it's an escape!*
JUDGE:	*Will someone please remove these unruly women from my courtroom!*

'That's more like it!' Daisy shouted from the back of the hall. 'That's just the ticket. Take ten minutes then we'll carry on. Two sugars in mine thanks.' She joined Rose and me, sitting about halfway back in the empty rows of seats and gave us a wink as she plonked herself down beside us.

Dorset Hall is a scruffy old place that the League have made their own. There are some cast iron radiators but even when they're on full blast and the pipes are rattling like a steam train, it's never warm. We were huddled in our coats, watching the rehearsal. Even wearing gloves and with my hands in my pockets, I was losing feeling in my fingers. But Daisy seemed impervious. She was running about in a cotton dress with her jacket swinging open, caught up in what she was doing, happy as Larry.

'Getting there, ain't it?'

'It's even better than last time,' smiled Rose.

'Handy to have the same cast. I'm glad Charlie agreed to it in the end.'

'She took some persuading,' I said.

'Understandable. But it's doing her good. I can see that.'

'I think it is.'

Daisy gave me a look.

'And what about you? Is this helping? Or hurting?'

A benefit performance to raise funds for Spain. In Harry's name. In his honour. When Sally from the League suggested it, I wanted to run away. As far and as fast as I could. Me and Charlie looked at each other and saw our fear reflected in each other's eyes. But it's what he would have wanted, money for his cause, so I agreed. Sometimes it's torture, like a knife twisting in an open wound. But once in a while, it's like he's here again, or close by, just out of sight. It's worth it for those moments.

'It's both,' I told her and she nodded and squeezed my arm.

'Thanks for helping us,' Rose said. 'Everyone is thrilled to have a professional involved.'

'Steady on! I'm just a chorus girl. And not so much of the girl these days—not by a long chalk!'

'But you never look any older.'

'If only! My middle-age spread is spreading nicely, thank you. I blame Humph's cooking.'

'How's he doing?' I asked, and her smile faded.

'Not so good since he had the 'flu last winter. It laid him low, he's still weak as a baby. Doesn't get out much, bless him. Couldn't come here, the cold would finish him off. Still, there's always an upside.' She brightened again. 'He bakes. And I eat. Speaking of which, where's my tea and biscuits?'

She patted my hand and headed for the kitchenette in the corner of the room.

'She's worried about him,' Rose said.

'It's the gas damage taking its toll.'

'Still paying the price.'

'Aye.'

There was a crash from the swing doors at the back of the hall.

'Every time!' Daisy shouted, coming back into the room with a mug of tea in one hand and a pile of biscuits in the other.

'Sorry, Daisy.'

I turned when I heard the voice. Tom Willis was making his way to us, between the chairs, the same lad we'd known for years, who had sat at our table many a time and who went to Spain with Harry but came back alone. He was still cheery and hearty, still full of good nature, but his face was older, full of things he'd seen and couldn't forget. He had brought Harry's belongings home to us, told us what it was like there, sparing our feelings even when we asked for the agonising truth. But me and Rose have seen war. We knew what he wasn't telling us, what he sees when he closes his eyes.

'How's it going?' he asked.

'Just about to start again,' said Daisy. 'So try not to fall over anything.'

He gave her a grin as she passed him.

'Chilly in here,' he said as he reached us. He wrapped his scarf around his neck, sitting in the row behind us and leaning forward, his arms on the back of our chairs.

'I think I've got frostbite.' Rose shivered and drew her coat

even more tightly around her. 'They must be freezing.' She nodded towards the stage where the cast were hovering in a group.

Catching Charlie's eye, Tom gave her a wave and she raised
a hand in response.

'How is she?' he asked.

'Getting stronger.'

'Good. That's good.'

He had witnessed her horror and anger before they went to
Spain and her crushing grief when he came back alone. I could
see guilt in his eyes and uncertainty. He wasn't sure that he was
forgiven. Or that he ever would be.

'Are you sorry you went?' I asked him once.

'No. Not for a minute.'

'But Spain is Franco's now. You lost.'

'We had to try.'

I wanted to scream at him. Why? For what? For nothing.
Nothing but pain. It's alright for you. You came back. Why
didn't you die instead of Harry? Why isn't my boy sitting here
mourning you? I wanted to, but I didn't. Because they were terrible, unforgivable thoughts. And because it wasn't alright for
him. We both knew that.

LIZZIE: *They're taking us to a ship at Woolwich. Two hundred
           and fifty miles on top of a coach in October. It won't be
           pleasant.*

HANNAH: *On top of the coach?*

LIZZIE: *Aye.*

HANNAH: *For all to see?*

LIZZIE: *Aye.*

HANNAH: *And shackled?*

LIZZIE: *It's orders.*

HANNAH: *Oh God!*

LIZZIE: *You'll hold your head high, Hannah. You've nothing to
           be ashamed of.*

HANNAH: *Why would God let this happen? Is he testing me? Is he
           punishing me? I don't understand!*

LIZZIE: *Hannah love, I'm not the person to talk to you about God,
           you know that. But I tell you now that nothing you have
           done has caused this misery. None of it is your doing. Do
           you hear me?*

147

HANNAH: *I want my family.*
LIZZIE: *I know, lass.*
HANNAH: *I'm not you, Lizzie. You're stronger than me.*
LIZZIE: *One foot in front of the other, lass. Remember that.*
HANNAH: *They say the voyage is living hell! There's many as don't survive it.*
LIZZIE: *We might find we got a death sentence after all!*
HANNAH: *Why didn't we? The Judge had no sympathy for us, that was clear enough.*
LIZZIE: *I've heard they need women in the colonies—that there's ten men to every woman in New South Wales.*
HANNAH: *So we're to be whores for the government?*
LIZZIE: *Well I doubt His Honour Justice Park would put it like that but aye, that's the truth of it.*
HANNAH: *The other side of the world.*
LIZZIE: *Don't be afraid.*
HANNAH: *Aren't you?*
LIZZIE: *'Course I am. But maybe it's a new start.*
HANNAH: *As a convict?*
LIZZIE: *I know that. I know we're prisoners and it might be worse there than what we've had so far, but there's a chance it might be better too, isn't there? There's a chance. Where there wasn't one before. Think of that.*
HANNAH: *You never give up hope, do you?*
LIZZIE: *What else is there?*

Hope. It's always the same and we never learn. Hope leads to broken dreams, to Peterloo and Gallipoli, to defeated workers and strikers that don't stand a chance. Hope leads to boys dead in foreign fields. Hope kills.

'I'm going home,' I said to Rose.

'Are you alright?'

'Headache,' I lied.

'I'll come with you.'

'No. You stay.'

She nodded, her face troubled. I walked past Tom, avoided Daisy's eyes and made my escape. It was going dark outside and the streetlights were glowing yellow in the twilight. I tried to steady my breathing, but rage was hammering in my head and chest. Hannah lost hope. Stopped believing. She walked into a

148

river in Australia with rocks in her pockets. I stood on the pavement and looked up at the moon, pale and ghostly behind a patch of cloud, and fought the urge to howl at the sky.

*

'There'll be another war. Nothing surer.'

Ellen was just back from Europe where she'd been part of an all-women delegation to Spain. She'd sneaked into Germany too, though she was officially banned there, as an undesirable.

'I'm not Hitler's favourite person. Franco's neither. I tell you, those two bastards and Mussolini too, they won't stop till we make them stop. Franco is raining bombs on undefended villages every day. I nearly choked with anger, seeing what he's doing. I felt so helpless. And our pathetic government won't lift a finger.' She drained her cup and held it out for a refill, still talking whilst Rose obliged. 'They can see what's happening to the Jews in Germany as well and they still do nothing. Mind you, there's more than one or two of them quite sympathetic to the Fuhrer's agenda. Some of the ruling class have always been Nazis, by inclination if not by name. Look at our abdicated king and his wife, all smiles with Hitler in Germany.'

She leaned back in her chair, cradling her cup in both hands. Her pixie face was pale and drawn. She looked exhausted and even smaller than usual. Truth is, she hadn't looked well for nearly a year, ever since the Jarrow March, when desperate, hungry men from her constituency walked three hundred miles to London, to be patronised and sent home by the government. All they got for their efforts was a suspension of their unemployment pay. Ellen was broken by it.

'They murdered that town and the people in it,' she said to me, through tears. 'It's evil.'

Something died in her after that, a light went out. But she kept working, she never stopped. Yet she had found time to be guest of honour at our end-of-year prize day and give a rousing speech to thirty wide-eyed girls.

'You are the future,' she told them. 'You are immensely lucky to be at this school, to get a radical education, encouraged to strive and be the best you can be. You owe to it others who are held back by class or sex, to beat on the closed doors until they open, push the boundaries until they break.'

She talked to them afterwards and signed their books. She met parents and shook their hands, made small talk and had her photograph taken. At last we managed to get her away and, as the girls went out with their families for celebration teas, we sat her down in the kitchen and put the kettle on.

'Thanks for that Ellen,' I said, as the water boiled. 'We really appreciate it.'

'My pleasure.' Her face was suddenly serious. She leaned across and took my hand. 'When I was in Spain, I went to Jarama.'

My heart twisted. Rose moved to stand behind my chair, her hand on my shoulder.

'There's no way of knowing where he is, where any of them are. But I stood in the valley and paid my respects.'

I couldn't speak. I pressed her hand and reached for Rose. I can never stand at his grave, I thought, as the kettle whistled.

The door opened and Charlie came in, carrying a plate of scones.

'Mrs Parker sent these.'

She put them on the table and took the kettle off the stove. Silence descended again as she made the tea. Rose was still at my side. I felt her make the effort to talk and was grateful that I didn't have to.

'You must have one of these, Ellen. You remember Annie Parker who won the Maths prize? Her parents work for us now. They live in the Lodge. And it turns out Mrs Parker has magical skills as a baker.'

Charlie fetched plates, butter and jam and sat next to Ellen. She had cut her hair short and it suited her. Her bright blue dress matched her eyes. She was beginning to look herself again as the weight of her grief shifted with time. Almost like the old Charlie. Almost.

'I enjoyed your speech, Miss Wilkinson.'

'It's Ellen, please. I'm glad to be here.'

'You inspired the girls.'

'That was the plan.'

Charlie sat forward.

'Is it very bad in Europe? What do you think will happen?'

And the war talk began, over tea and scones. It seems Spain was the first of many battles and them in charge here won't be able to keep their heads in the sand much longer. A new generation will march out to kill or be killed, in the name of whatever. All that's certain is the arms trade will flourish and a few very rich men will get even richer. And millions will feel the pain that still rips at my heart, however much time passes.

'It's not like the last war,' Ellen said, as if she could read my thoughts. 'These Fascists have to be stopped. Granted, they should have been stopped before they got this powerful, but now they are, we have to fight and win. We have to.'

Anger swept through me again like a high tide. My cup clattered into its saucer.

'But we don't win, do we? We never win.'

Charlie's eyes widened, and Ellen looked at me like I'd kicked her. Rose, still at my shoulder, put a hand to my hair.

'We won the vote,' she said quietly. 'You and Ellen, and Daisy and Sylvia and all the others. You won it.'

'And what did it change? Complacent men are still in charge, running things in their own interest. The rich still get richer and the poor still suffer.'

I knew it was sacrilege to talk that way in this company, but I couldn't stop myself. Rose held onto me, like she was saving me from drowning. I suppose, in a way, she was. I waited for Ellen to read me the riot act, but it wasn't her that spoke, it was Charlie. She sat up straight in her chair and there was something new in her face, something learned the hard way.

'Ellen is an MP,' she said. 'Twenty years ago, we didn't have the vote and now there are women in Parliament. And there'll be more. It will be painfully slow, there'll be two steps forward and one step back, but we'll persist.' She smiled at me. 'You taught me that, Nora. You and Rose. To do anything else would betray Harry. I haven't got his courage and I let him down when he needed me, but I'll never do it again.'

'That's right,' Ellen slapped the table. 'We keep going.'

'However long it takes.'

I felt a million miles away from them. I saw their shared sense of purpose and remembered how it used to feel, but I couldn't summon anything like it. I was empty. Rose was looking at me with her heart in her eyes. She knew what I was feeling. We've fought the fight together for years but this time the price is too high. I can't just pay it and move on. I can't move on.

151

*

Over twenty years since I left Salford and every time I come back, I look for changes and find none. Same factories, same cramped streets, same dirt, same rain. Chimneys belching smoke, soot on every surface, grit on the cobbles. There are slums all over the country, you don't have to walk far from Ealing Common to see filth and poverty, but Salford has a dismal misery all its own. Or maybe I'm just biased. I can't walk to Mam and Dad's front door without remembering the dark, freezing mornings, the clogs and shawls, the clattering looms and spinning bobbins, the mixture of boredom and weariness as the long hours dragged by. I lived for the end of the shift, for meetings and rallies and glimpses of a better life. Is that why I went to war? Just to be somewhere else? Maybe all my fine feelings were nothing more than an excuse to run away.

I was tempted to flee again, standing in the street, looking at the door knocker, dreading the conversations to come. I'd rehearsed the lies for their benefit, but I knew they wouldn't be taken in. There's no fooling Grace Barnes, she could always see right through me.

Dad answered the door, still a tall man, even stooped with age. Mam's head barely reaches his shoulder, like Rose and me. At singalongs, after a beer or two, he'd give us his party piece — 'It's a great big shame' — and Mam would shake her head and smile.

Nagging at a fellow that is six foot three
And her only four foot two.

'I'm five foot three,' she'd say, every time, and he'd deliver the punchline, on cue.

'Never marry a radical, whatever size she is! Not if you want a quiet life.'

It was all for show. He never wanted a quiet life. Just as well, cos he never got one. He'd escape to his allotment when it got too much for him, but that wasn't often. He was never happier than when the house was full of comrades and fighting talk, with Mam at the centre, pouring tea and raising spirits.

His face lit up when he saw me on the doorstep.

'She's here, Grace,' he called over his shoulder, before stepping back to let me into the narrow hallway. He took me by the shoulders and looked into my eyes. 'How's it going, lass?'

Before I had a chance to answer, Mam came out of the kitchen, wiping her hands on a dish towel. She had the same question in her face, the same love and anxiety. I hadn't seen them since Harry's memorial. It's easier to lie at a distance. Standing next to them, I couldn't pretend. Something broke inside and for the first time in months, the tears came. They both moved in to hold me and the three of us stood in a huddle in the dim little hall, clinging to the wreckage in a tide of grief.

It was Mam who moved first.

'I've set tea in the parlour. Jim, get that drop of brandy from the cupboard. We could all do with a nip.'

She took my hand and led me through to the best chair, in front of the fire. I felt like a little girl again, bringing my sorrows home to be heard and mended. I took a cup of tea and let them lace it with brandy and sugar, sipping it as they drank their own, sitting side by side on the settee, waiting for me to speak, waiting patiently till I was ready.

'He died for nothing', I said at last. 'Threw his life away for nowt. For a foolish dream that I fed him.'

'Nay, lass,' dad shook his head. 'You can't blame yourself.'

'I can. I do.'

Mam put her cup down. The parlour was tiny and our knees were almost touching as she leaned towards me.

'That foolish dream you talk about, we fed it to you. So do you blame us too?'

'It doesn't matter. It won't bring him back.'

'No it won't. But that's why the dream matters more than ever.'

I shook my head.

'I don't believe that any more.'

I knew my words would hurt them, but I couldn't help it. I could see they were shaken. Despite everything, it made me smile to think they hadn't batted an eyelid when I came home unmarried and pregnant, with Rose at my side, but this, they wouldn't stand for.

'What's funny?' asked Mam.

I took her hand.

'Have I ever thanked you properly for accepting me and Rose?'

'No need.'

'No need at all,' said Dad.

'Most people would say different.'

'Aye.' Mam rubbed my fingers, like she used to when I was little, and it was cold. 'Well, since when have we thought like most people?' She stood up. 'Come on. We're going out.'

'Where?'

'There's summat you need to see.'

I didn't want to go anywhere but there's no point resisting Grace Barnes. As she put her hat and coat on I threw Dad a look and he smiled.

'Your Mam's right.'

'You always say that. You coming?'

'Aye, I'll join you.'

'Where are we going?'

'You'll know soon enough.'

We walked through the familiar streets together, past women in pinnies, kneeling at the front step with a bucket and donkey stone, kids kicking a ball on a scrubby patch of grass between the houses and washing flapping above the cobbles in back alleys. Two decades since this was my world and it felt like yesterday. Where does the time go?

'Here we are,' said Mam at last, stopping in front of a big brick building with rows of windows and steps up to the front door. I knew what it was and stared at her and Dad in surprise.

'The Friends' Meeting House? Are you Quakers now?'

'It's being used as a school. Come on.'

Mam led the way inside, to the main hall. We stood outside the door and looked in. There were rows of desks set out and about thirty boys and girls sitting in front of a young woman teacher who was writing on a blackboard. The children were different ages, from about six to twelve, it looked to me. They were well dressed, clothes clean and shoes polished. The girls had ribbons in their hair. At a sign from the teacher, they started to clear their desks and stand up. Lessons were over for the day.

'What are we doing here?'

The door opened and the children streamed out. There was

154

the usual pushing and shoving, laughing and shouting. Then I realised. They were speaking Spanish.

'Hello, Felipe,' Mam said to one of the boys at the front.

'Hello, Mrs Barnes,' he replied in accented English. 'Hello, Mr Barnes.'

'Where's your sister?' Dad asked.

Felipe turned and pointed to a small girl in the crowd. She smiled with delight when she saw them and pushed her way through to the front.

'Hola! Senor Barnes!'

'English, Elena,' her brother said sternly as she ran to Dad and gave him a hug.

Over her shiny, bobbed hair, Dad gave me a smile.

'She's besotted with your dad,' Mum said.

Felipe was looking at me with curiosity.

'I'm Nora,' I told him. 'Pleased to meet you, Felipe.'

'Hello.'

The teacher appeared in the doorway.

'Hurry up, you two,' she said to Felipe and Elena. 'Mrs Lane is waiting to take you back for tea.'

'You come, Senor Barnes?' asked Elena.

'Aye. We'll see you later. Off you go now.' Dad peeled her off his arm and handed her to her brother. They ran along the corridor to the main entrance, Elena waving all the way, till they turned the corner and disappeared.

I looked at Mam and Dad and they looked at me. Basque refugees. I knew that the government had finally given way to public pressure and let some children in, but not that there were any in Salford.

'They're in the Memorial Orphanage on Seedley Road,' Mam answered my unspoken question. 'It's temporary. They have to go back as soon as it's considered safe.'

'And there's no money provided for them,' said the teacher. 'Everything is given by volunteers.'

Dad pressed my arm.

'This is Miss Reynolds. She's a Spanish language student at the University.'

'It's Sheila,' she held out a hand and I took it. 'And you must be Nora. Will you come for tea? Meet the children properly?'

'We have to,' Dad said. 'I promised.'

Sheila and me walked in front of Mam and Dad on the narrow pavement. She was even younger close up, with freckles on her nose and earnest brown eyes behind her big glasses. She shot a few quick looks at me from under her hat and there was a look on her face I've seen a lot lately. She was wondering whether to mention Harry or not, the dilemma of being faced with the grief of a stranger. I headed her off before she said anything, made it easier on the both of us.

'They look happy. Settled.'

'Yes.' She relaxed a bit. 'They've adjusted well.'

'It's good to see.'

'For a while, we kept finding food in their pockets at night. They couldn't believe that more would be coming on a regular basis.' Her eyes darkened. 'Most of them are from Guernica. What they went through—'

I'd seen the pictures. A small market town firebombed into charred rubble by the Luftwaffe, in support of Franco. A taste of what the Fascists can and will do, was Ellen's verdict. A trial run.

'Loud noises frightened them,' she went on. 'Lots of bad dreams and wet beds.'

'And now look at them,' I said, and she smiled at last.

'You run a school, don't you?'

'For older girls.'

'Your mother told me about it. I think it's wonderful work you're doing.'

'So are you.'

'We have to do what we can, don't we?'

We reached the orphanage and walked up the drive to the big house set back from the road in its own corner plot. It was a grim old building outside, hemmed in with tall dark trees but once through the doors, it was a different place altogether. Volunteers had cleaned and polished, put down bright rugs and hung colourful curtains. The dormitories had yellow walls and rows of beds with matching blue covers, there were toys and books and the smell of baking in the corridors. All done out of the goodness of people's hearts. Just to help. True, there were some saying what about the kids all over Salford living in slums and going hungry? Shouldn't we worry about our own before taking in foreigners? What happens when their families want to join

them? What then? Where does it end? They're right about looking after our own. Course we should. But giving these traumatised kids a few healing months has to be the right thing to do.
And whether it's done or not, the poor of Salford, and everywhere else, will continue to struggle and starve. That's a whole
different argument.

'Senor Barnes!' Elena appeared from nowhere and flung herself at Dad.

He held out both hands in front of him, palms down, fingers
clenched. I had a flashback to childhood, when he would do this
for me. Guess which hand. Find the sweet. Getting it right was
as exciting as getting the treat. Elena was laughing, her little face
lit up with pleasure. She chose his right hand. It was empty. Of
course, he gave her the sweet anyway. She knew he would, just
like I always knew. That wasn't the point.

There was a sudden commotion in a room across the hall,
scuffling feet and raised voices. Sheila strode off and we followed her. A group of older boys were standing together, faces
flushed and defiant. One of them was holding a length of rough
twig from the garden with what looked like an old scarf tied to
the end. A crimson scarf. They had made a red flag.

'Give it to me now, son.' Father Geoghan from St Luke's was
standing in front of them, holding out his hand. 'We can't have
that in here.'

The volunteers were a mixed bunch, including some from the
Catholic Protection Society. We aren't Catholic and were never
church-goers anyway, but everyone knew old Father Geoghan,
with his untidy white hair and stains on his crumpled cassock.
He was kind, always ready to help out. I wasn't surprised to see
him there.

'What's the matter, Father?' Sheila looked from the boys to
the priest, her face puzzled.

I noticed Felipe was in the group. He saw Mam and Dad and
called out.

'It is ours. Our flag.'

'It's Communism,' said Father Geoghan. 'It's godless.'

The boy holding it raised his arm and waved it over his head.

'People with this flag helped us. Church helped Franco.'

As Sheila stood helplessly in the middle of the confrontation,
more of the children joined the boys as others crowded in the

doorway to watch. The sight of the flag seemed to draw them together, a shared experience, a group memory that was a thing apart from this bright room in a foreign country.

'These children have been misled,' said the priest. 'It is our duty to lead them back to the right path.'

'No Pasaran!' shouted the boy with the flag and the others joined in till the room was ringing with it.

Mam moved forward and took Father Geoghan's arm, steering him to the door. As we followed, the chanting stopped and a cheer went up. I heard Sheila settling them down as we left. The drama was over. Mam was bustling round the old priest, getting him a cup of tea and a piece of cake. He was more distressed than angry. Catholics and Communism don't mix.

'The flag means something to them, Father.' She stirred sugar into his cup. 'Protection. Solidarity. After what they've been through.'

'There are better symbols.'

Over his head, Mam caught my eye. Not for me, her face said. None better for me. She walked to my side and took my arm, smiling up at me from her five foot three.

'Out of the mouths of babes,' she said. 'We fight Fascists. Whether we win or lose, we fight them. There's no other way.'

1945

IT was raining but no-one cared. Barrage balloons still hovered, huge and silver, over the bombed-out buildings. Sandbags were still piled under cross-taped windows. Searchlights still pierced the sky above rows of suburban gardens, dug for victory. But tonight, there were no planes to pick out in the dark and the bright beams were for celebration, not protection. The Anderson shelters and the underground stations were empty, there was no wail of sirens, no drone of planes, no whump of exploding rockets, no fires, no terror, no death. Not tonight. It was VE Day and all over the country, people were drunk with joy and gin and light-headed with relief. Crowds were dancing in the streets, strangers were wrapped around each other like lovers and there was bunting everywhere, miles of bunting that had appeared from nowhere, draped over shop fronts and statues and the jagged remains of ruined homes. Soldiers, sailors and airmen were wandering in gangs, handing out cigarettes from their kit-bags, swinging from lamp-posts and singing. Everybody was singing.

Tom and I were sitting on the edge of the fountain in Trafalgar Square. He was in his air force blues and I was wearing my best suit and my last pair of nylons. I had curled my hair and painted my lips with beetroot juice, in the long absence of lipstick. We were passing a bottle of beer between us and watching the celebrations. Neither of us wanted to join the throngs at the Palace, hip-hooraying the royals and Churchill, so we had wandered through the West End and found ourselves in the jubilant masses around Nelson's Column. The rain had stopped for the moment, the night was warm, for May, and a few stars were breaking through the clouds. It felt dreamlike, not quite real. But the joy all around was contagious.

You could barely see the lions, there were so many revellers sitting on them and below, somehow, a beer wagon had made its way into the sea of people, piled with barrels and a group of cheering soldiers sitting astride them. Half a dozen very drunk girls were splashing about in the water behind us and a couple of brave souls had climbed into the basin at the top, waving flags and shouting. I couldn't hear what they said. There was so much noise, I couldn't hear Tom, even when he put his mouth to my ear and bellowed. I smiled at him and shook my head and he grinned and kissed me instead. It was nice. When he pulled away, his eyes were questioning, uncertain of my reaction, but he relaxed when I put my arms around his neck. I leaned into him, enjoying the bulk of him, his strong body, his warmth. Why not? It was VE Day. So, we held hands as he walked me back to Cadogan Square.

'When will you be demobbed?' I asked him as we made our way through the riotous streets.

'Apparently it all starts in six weeks. So any time after that.'

'Then what?'

He shrugged and laughed.

'I've no idea. Normal life seems like a distant memory.'

We were passing a block of bombed-out flats. The front wall had gone, but the staircases were still intact, zig-zagging from floor to floor. Some of the rooms were still furnished. At the top, there was one with a bed, a wardrobe and a chest of drawers, roses on the wallpaper and a rag rug on the floor. It was like a doll's house, waiting for the façade to be clicked back into place, except for the mounds of blasted rubble and twisted metal it sat in. Normal life? What was that?

'You should run for Parliament,' I said. 'You'd do a great job.'

'My grandfather was an MP for fifteen years.'

'I didn't know that.'

'I don't advertise it. He was a Tory.'

'All the more reason to do it. Redress the balance.'

'That would be a big job. His life's work was opposing the Trade Union Act.'

'Oh dear.'

'He was a mine owner. Dirty money, in every sense.'

I squeezed his hand.

'Inherited wealth is rarely clean, is it? Ours was from slum rents.' We got to my door and I faced him. 'Be an MP and assuage both our consciences.'

'Alright,' he laughed. 'As you insist.'

'I do.'

'Can I take a year or two to have a life first?'

'Shirker.'

He bent his head and kissed me again. I climbed up a step, to be nearer his height and his arms went around me, our bodies close, his hands in my hair.

'Are you coming in?' I asked.

'Your parents?'

'In the country for the duration.'

'You've been living here alone?'

'Not exactly. There are a lot of homeless people in London.'

He pulled away, surprise in his face.

'You've been putting them up?'

'As many as I could. A drop in the ocean.'

'And your parents don't mind?'

'Are you coming in or not?'

'Charlie? They don't know, do they?'

'I think they suspect. They don't really care. They don't care about much since Miles was killed.'

He was on The Hood and died in the cold waters of the Denmark Strait. He was twenty-six, a year younger than I am now. I'm not his little sister any more. My parents seem to be not so much bereaved as bewildered by his loss. I rushed round to Cadogan Square when the news came, stayed with them, tried to be a daughter, all the time avoiding the helpless questions in their eyes. I wanted to go back to Ealing, to my life at the school. Rose, Nora and I joined the Red Cross when the war started, and it felt wrong to miss my shifts but my parents seemed so lost, I couldn't leave them.

I moved back into my childhood bedroom, feeling the chasm that had opened in the five years of my absence, between my life then and who I am now. My parents seemed like strangers and I'm sure they felt the same about me. We ate our meals together and sat in the drawing room behind the blackout curtains, with the wireless filling the silence that always hovered between us. As the bombing raids increased, we spent more and more time huddled in their shelter. I'd read to them, by torchlight. All their favourites. Tennyson, Browning, Kipling.

If you can force your heart and nerve and sinew
To serve your turn long after they are gone,
And so hold on when there is nothing in you
Except the will which says to them: 'Hold on!'

Sometimes I'd look up to find them holding hands under the blankets they were wrapped in, or sleeping sitting up, heads together against the corrugated iron wall and the words on the pages in my hands would blur as the tears came to my eyes.

One morning they announced, out of the blue, that they were going to the country house and would live there till the war was over. Would I stay in Cadogan Square and look after the place? I agreed readily enough, ashamed at the relief that washed over me. After I waved them off a few days later with promises to visit, I stood in the hall for a long, still moment. The sense of myself that had dissipated, since I stepped back through the door behind me, re-formed in the sudden quiet of the empty house. I breathed it in and smiled. I could take up where I left off. I could split my time between Knightsbridge and Ealing. I could be useful again.

'I'm sorry about your brother.' Tom brushed a stray curl from my eyes.

'I used to tell him he'd never grow up but that's not what I meant.'

He looked up at the opulent building behind us.

'Quite a lodging house you're running.'

'It will all come to me now, so what's the difference?'

'At least you're back in touch with your folks. That's something.'

'The war put things into perspective.'

'Yes.'

I leaned into him and took his hand.

'And now, Tom, my dear, do you want to stand chatting on the doorstep all night, or do you want to come upstairs with me?'

162

He stopped talking then.

Later, as we lay curled together in my childhood bed, he kissed my bare shoulder and laughed softly.

Well, that was unexpected.'

'Was it? Really?'

'You're very direct these days.'

'I've grown up.'

'I like it.'

I pushed back the sheet and he reached for me.

'Don't get up.'

'I'm not. Just a minute.' I walked to the window and pulled the hated blackout curtain aside. The room was suddenly awash with a silver glow and I turned back to look at him. He was lounging back on my pillows, his skin pale, the sheet wrapped around his hips almost luminous in the moonlight. 'You look like a Grand Master painting, lying there.'

'Well that's something I never thought I'd hear.'

'Just take the compliment.'

'Very well. Thank you.'

I leant on the sill and gazed up at the sky.

'I've missed the moon.'

'May I remind you, Miss West, that you are standing in the window, completely naked.'

'So I am.'

He held out his arms and I got back into bed, nestling in the warmth of him. We held each other in the moonlight and I felt his breath in my hair. Somewhere in the distance, there was still singing.

When the lights go on again, all over the world.
And the boys are home again, all over the world.

The war was over. For us. Japan was fighting on, Germany was starving and in ruins, Europe was bitter and divided, hundreds of thousands were mourning their dead, but our war was over. Hitler was cold in his bunker, Mussolini hanging from a lamp-post, Franco isolated in Spain. Fascism lost.

I looked up into Tom's face.

'Thank you for not dying.'

'You're welcome.'

'You thought I blamed you. For Harry. But I never did.'

'Survivor's guilt. I have a double dose now.'

'I let you both down.'

'No.'

'Yes. I've tried to make up for it since. But I did.'

'He never felt that.'

'How can you know?'

'I was there.' He propped himself on one elbow and looked down at me. 'Can we be direct again?'

'Yes.'

'You'll never love anyone like you loved Harry, will you?'

There was no point in dissembling. We both knew the answer. In the silence, I was surprised to see a smile in his eyes.

'What?'

'It's alright, old thing. Really. I'm happy with this, with whatever this is. I just wanted you to know that.'

'I don't know what this is.'

'Me neither.'

I kissed him, soft-lipped and open-mouthed and we rolled together as a burst of laughter and another song drifted up from the square outside.

JUNE 16TH

Today my parents celebrated their Ruby wedding anniversary and there was a party in the country. I tried every excuse I could think of to get out of attending but, in the end, conscience overpowered comfort. I drove from London in the summer sunshine and, with the top down and the wind in my hair, some of my dread was blown away, so that I arrived dishevelled but smiling to greet the crowd drinking Pimm's on the lawn.

'Charlotte—your hair—you look like a scarecrow, darling!' Mother hurried across to meet me. She was wearing a Schiaparelli dress in powder blue silk, bought in Paris before the war and still exquisite. 'And trousers?'

I had hoped I looked like Katherine Hepburn when I put them on and set out, but next to mother's practised elegance, I felt suddenly dowdy. I'm not good at dressing up, am never happier than when I'm in an old cardigan, but I had made an effort for my parents' sake. Clearly though, it was unsuccessful.

'Hello, Mother,' I patted at my head ineffectively. 'Happy Anniversary.'

'So this is Charlotte?' a small woman with a mild, kind face, held out a hand in greeting and I took it.

'It's Charlie,' I said, seeing Mother frown with disapproval. 'This is Mrs Trentham.'

'Oh, call me Dora, please. This is my husband George.'

George Trentham towered over his wife. He had a bald head, a white moustache and friendly brown eyes under bushy white brows. There was a small book in the pocket of his tweed jacket and I could just make out the title. *Stones of Venice*. I doubt if many people at my parents' parties read Ruskin. My interest was piqued.

'We've just moved to the village,' he smiled, shaking my hand. 'Bought The Laurels, the old place by the church.'

'Pleased to meet you. What brings you to Sussex?'

'Retirement.'

'George is an architect,' said Dora.

'Not any more. I'm going to walk on the cliffs and keep bees, like Sherlock Holmes.'

'Does that make me Dr Watson or Mrs Hudson?' Dora laughed and took his arm.

'Forgive me,' Mother stepped in. 'I'm going to steal Charlotte away for a moment.'

I was reluctant to leave their company. I liked them, which made them all but unique among my parents' friends. But mother was determined.

'It's Charlie,' I repeated as I was led away. Dora and George smiled, a little conspiratorially as I waved back at them and I made a note to seek them out later. 'Where are we going?'

'To find a hairbrush.'

I was tempted to resist but decided to concede defeat. Whoever said choose your battles gave wise advice.

'Where's Father?' I asked as we approached the terrace.

'In the summerhouse, smoking cigars with Dr Lockwood.'

'How is he?'

'He's fine. Absolutely fine.' But her face belied her words. He wasn't fine. Neither of them were. Four years since Miles died and the shock had worn off now but they still hadn't come to terms with it. Do we ever? Father, most of all, was diminished

165

by it. He couldn't comprehend how it was that his ordered world had shattered so completely. So it was Mother who, unexpectedly and movingly, battled on for the two of them, a daily insistence on normal life, for his protection. We barely agree on anything, but I realise that I've spent years underestimating my mother and that, like most of us, she too is driven by love.

'Mother—'

'Go in and tidy yourself darling. Don't dawdle.'

Some conversations are impossible.

I walked through the French windows into the drawing room. A small group of guests were gathered around the fireplace and they looked up and nodded. I gave them a smile, the best I could muster, but I didn't stop to make pleasantries. The Easterbrooks and the Wetherbys were local landowners, big fish in the small pond of rural Sussex, Masters of the Hunt and magistrates. We had nothing in common. I caught a few snippets of their conversation as I passed.

'Churchill didn't want a general election. He wanted the war coalition to continue.'

'But Labour insisted he go to the country.'

'They'll regret it.'

'Grubby little people.'

I ran for the hall. There was a large formal portrait of my grandparents in pride of place over the stairs and they looked down on me severely as I headed for my room. I always think of Woodlands as my grandparents' house, a place of childhood summers and family Christmases, hide and seek and nursery teas whilst the grown-ups dressed for dinner. With them gone, no matter how many times I visit, no matter how much my mother redecorates, it seems to me that we are trespassers, that it will always be theirs. These days I feel like an interloper whenever I'm with my family and their circle, but never more so than at Woodlands, with Grandpa's ghost at my shoulder.

'Thank God your grandfather didn't live to see this,' Father always says when my politics are under discussion and it's true enough that Grandpa would have been scandalised by how I live my life.

What Granny would have said or thought, I've no idea. I never once heard her give voice to an independent opinion on anything. Grandpa did her thinking for her and she really didn't seem to mind. I remember watching her face, waiting for a glimmer of resentment, longing for the slightest flicker of rebellion but I never saw it. She told me once that voting was unladylike. What a sin it is to close people's minds to themselves.

I tidied myself up, resisted the temptation to stay in my room a little longer and made my way back downstairs. The conversation by the fireplace hadn't improved.

'Anyone who doesn't vote for Churchill, after all he's done for the country, is an ungrateful wretch.'

'Attlee can't hold a candle to him. No charisma. He isn't a leader.'

'Beaverbrook's right. He's a miserable little man.'

I had turned towards them, taken a breath to begin speaking, but Mother stepped into the room just in time. She was caught in the sunlight standing there and I saw the lines in her face, the weariness in her eyes and my heart went out to her. She had lost both her children, in different ways. I should be married to an Easterbrook or a Wetherby, making her a grandmother, and Miles should be squandering his allowance and laughing fondly as she scolded him for his waywardness. The life she had expected would never be hers now. I crossed the room and hugged her, felt her stiffen with surprise before she submitted for the briefest moment. She made a small sound, an intake of breath, then pulled away, avoiding my eyes. She scanned the room quickly, keeping up appearances. Her laugh was embarrassed.

'How lovely, darling. Silly girl.' She turned back to the garden. 'Come and say hello to Daddy.'

I followed her out. The sun was warm and the garden was bright with colour. The lawn was green, the trees in full leaf. It was beautiful and comfortingly timeless. Standing there, the war felt like a distant memory, the rubble and ruins of London like another world. No wonder my parents and their friends found it so easy to ignore poverty and desperation when they were so far removed from it, when they could step out of their elegant homes into gardens like this. The world was theirs. I turned around and walked back.

'Charlotte?' Mother's voice followed me.

'You go on. I won't be long.'

'Did you hear Churchill's radio broadcast?' Mrs Easterbrook was saying. 'He said, if the Socialists win, they'll set up a

Gestapo here in England.'

'Yes, the newspapers are saying the same.'

'The Socialists don't like freedom. Look at Russia.'

'Russia is Communist,' I said. 'Not Socialist.'

They hadn't realised I'd reappeared. Every head turned in my direction.

'Same thing,' said Mr Wetherby. He was a red-faced man with a permanently affronted expression that was at its height as he looked at me.

'No, it isn't. And you obviously haven't noticed but Attlee has been running the country for years whilst Churchill lapped up the war glory.'

'Oh, I say!' Freddy Easterbrook, an old friend of Miles, was leaning on the fireplace, half-listening, but he woke up at that. 'Come on, old girl. Churchill just saved the country.'

'Oh yes, he cares about the country. Just not the people in it.' There was a rumble of disapproval but I ignored it and pressed on. 'Not the working people, anyway. When the Welsh miners were on strike he wanted to send in the troops. He said if they were hungry, we should fill their bellies with lead.'

Freddy, to his credit, looked shocked.

'Did he? Well that's rotten.'

'He accuses Labour of Fascism, but he was the one who supported Mussolini and called Hitler a great man.'

'A lot of people were fooled by Hitler.' Mrs Wetherby was what everyone called a real countrywoman. She spent her life in tweeds, loved horses and dogs and shotguns. She was no-nonsense but good natured and I had always quite liked her. But I didn't spare her. I wasn't in the mood.

'And a lot of people never were. The Socialists saw him for what he was, and fought him, whilst Churchill and the government did nothing. The man I loved went to fight the Fascists in Spain and was killed doing it. How many Labour party members have just finished six years fighting the Nazis? How many will never come back? Churchill and Beaverbrook should be ashamed of what they said. They should be ashamed of themselves.'

I was fighting tears as they stared at me in silence. I didn't pride myself for a second that I had made an impression, they were just embarrassed by my outburst. I had broken the rules, by caring. It was Freddy who finally broke the tension.

'Come on, old girl.' He detached himself from the fireplace. 'Let's get a drink.'

I let him lead me into the garden. Behind us, I knew, his family and the Wetherbys were breathing a sigh of relief and raising their eyebrows.

'You rescued me, Freddy, my dear. I'm grateful.'

'You rather went off the deep-end, didn't you?' He handed me a glass of Pimm's.

'I'm not sorry.'

'I didn't know that stuff. About Churchill.'

'There's a lot more.'

'I'm sorry for your loss. I didn't know that either.'

'No. Well, my parents liked to pretend that Harry didn't exist. And now he doesn't.'

'Miles too.'

'And so many more.'

'Yes.'

The conversation was petering out. I saw the Trenthams close by and waved them over.

'Freddy, do you know Dora and George?'

'Yes, we've met. Hello again.'

'We've been hearing a lot about you, Charlie.' George beamed down at me.

'Not all good, I'm sure.'

Dora patted my shoulder.

'I was the black sheep of the family too. I wanted to go on the stage. My father, the Reverend, was unimpressed!'

'And did you?'

'I joined a Pierrot troupe in Eastbourne.'

'I knew I liked you, Dora!'

'It lasted all of six days. Then I was found and escorted home. My one big adventure.'

'Apart from your marriage.' George nudged her, and she smiled at him.

'If you say so, dear.'

'I wouldn't mind trying out for the pictures,' grinned Freddy. 'The next Errol Flynn. What do you think?'

'More like Boris Karloff.'

'Charming! That's what I get for rescuing you from your social catastrophes.'

Dora and George looked at me enquiringly and I gave them a rueful smile.

'I gave a political lecture to an unwilling audience.'

'Ah.'

'She did a hatchet job on Churchill,' said Freddy. 'To the Chairman of the local Conservative Association.'

'What?'

'Henry Wetherby.'

'Is he? I had no idea.'

'You don't like Churchill then?' asked George.

'No. Sorry.'

'Don't apologise to us. We're Liberals.'

'That's an improvement, isn't it, old girl?'

'Well,' I said, 'it's a start.'

Dora laughed.

'Do you plan to convert us?'

'I plan to try.'

'Isn't it a wasted vote, for the Liberals?' asked Freddy. 'They can never win.'

'Freddy—that's an intelligent question!'

'I have my moments.'

'You're right, Freddy,' said George. 'But old habits die hard. Can Labour win, Charlie? Do you really think so?'

I hesitated.

'A lot of people on the doorsteps tell us they're ready for change. They won't have a repeat of the last war, when the soldiers came back to poverty and hunger.'

'I suppose, in a way, rationing has given everyone a taste of equality.'

'And they're asking why that shouldn't always be the case.'

'But?' George asked, and I looked up into his face and shook my head.

'It seems too much to ask that the country will turn its back on Churchill.'

'Yes.'

'He has the papers and the BBC on his side too,' said Dora. 'All that propaganda.'

'The establishment protecting its own.'

'Right. Now you've lost me.' Freddy threw up his hands.

'Ellen Wilkinson says the only person she knows who really

believes in the possibility of victory is Nye Bevan.'

'It would be extraordinary.'

'No chance,' said Freddy. 'Not a hope.'

'Oh, there's always hope, Freddy,' I said. 'Even if sometimes, that's all there is.'

Dora and George were all smiles.

'Well said, Charlie.' Dora squeezed my arm. 'Are there more like you in Labour?'

'Lots. Have I piqued your interest?'

'Perhaps you have.'

'Charlotte—' It was Mother, calling to me across the lawn.

'I'm sorry,' I said. 'I'd better go.'

'Yes, of course.'

'Game of croquet later?' asked Freddy.

'Yes, why not.'

Dora called after me as I left.

'I think the trousers look lovely.'

I gave her a smile, which faded as I got closer to Mother and saw the expression on her face. I braced myself. News, it seems, travels fast.

'How could you?' she said as I reached her. 'These people are our guests, our friends.'

'I'm sorry.'

'Couldn't you bite your tongue, just once? For one day?'

She was right. Her friends were spoilt and complacent, but, this time, she was right.

'I know. It's your day. I was wrong.' I was genuinely contrite. 'Should I apologise?' It would kill me to do it, but if that's what it took. 'I am sorry. Truly.'

Mother shook her head.

'I don't know, Charlotte. If you didn't look just like my mother, I'd suspect you were a changeling. I'm at a loss to know how your father and I produced you.'

'I must be a throwback. I'll bet there was a West at Watt Tyler's side in the Peasants' Revolt.'

I grinned and her face softened for a moment.

'Come and see your father.'

Surprisingly, that seemed to be that. I know she will never understand my politics, never approve of them, but as I followed her to the summerhouse, I felt that somehow, something had shifted. Perhaps she realised that I loved her, despite everything, as she loved me. Whatever it was, it seemed we had reached a level of acceptance that was more than I had ever hoped for and I felt lighter, knowing it.

'I'm glad I came,' I said to her back, but she was waving to a young couple in the rose garden and didn't hear me.

JULY 26TH

Nye Bevan was right and everyone else was wrong.

There were three weeks between the ballot and the result, to allow for the votes of the services overseas, then, today at nine o'clock the boxes were opened and counted, and after all the speeches and all the cigars, after Dunkirk, the Battle of Britain and D-Day, after the victory parades and the waving from open-topped cars, the voters sent Churchill packing. It was a Labour landslide.

'Charlie!' Tom came bounding up the stairs at Cadogan Square. 'Charlie, have you heard?'

I was still in my dressing gown, glued to the wireless. A Labour gain, the announcer said. And another. And another. Prominent Tories were losing their seats, going down like ninepins, Macmillan, Bracken and Randolph Churchill among them. Tom was red-cheeked with excitement, his face one big grin. I ran to him and we waltzed around the room, wide-eyed with amazement and joy.

'We did it, old girl,' he beamed at me. 'We did it!'

A few weeks ago, we would have celebrated by falling onto my bed, but the fling had been short-lived and we didn't do that anymore, by mutual consent.

'It was our delayed rebound,' Tom said. 'From Harry.'

He was wiser than he looked.

'Just dear friends then?'

'Always.'

Nonetheless, in my elation, I considered leading him astray one last time, but he forestalled me.

'Hurry up and get dressed. Let's get to HQ.'

So, I threw on some clothes and we rushed down to the local Labour Hall, where the celebrations were in full swing. Comrades were whooping and laughing and dancing on the tables and every face was alive with joy. It was like VE day all over again.

A few weeks ago, at the party conference in Blackpool, Ellen Wilkinson had made a rousing speech.

'We are fighting the party of big business,' she said to the packed hall. 'The party that controls the great industries, the cartels and the press. These are our enemies. The world we want to see cannot be built on the shifting foundations of their crony capitalism.'

Nora, Rose and I were sitting together in the audience, Ellen's guests for the day. It was the biggest conference in Labour's history and the atmosphere was alive with anticipation and a sense of possibility. We had fought another war and this time there was no going back to the same old unjust world. Change was coming. It was in every face around me. Even Nora was daring to believe again. I could see it in her eyes.

'We are the builders,' roared Nye Bevan from the platform. 'We have been the dreamers. We have been the sufferers.' And as the hall erupted, we jumped to our feet and applauded and cheered with the rest.

'We can do it,' I said to Rose and Nora on the train home. 'We beat Hitler. We can build a Welfare State.'

But we never believed it would happen so soon. The obstacles were too great, the opposition too powerful. We would work towards the next General Election, make slow and steady progress and in five years or so, we'd see victory. That was the plan. But the plan went wrong. Wonderfully and beautifully wrong.

At HQ, Miriam Freedman, the branch secretary, put down the telephone and shouted to the room.

'Churchill isn't at his own count. He's sent his wife.'

'He'll be with his team,' said Tom. 'Weighing his options.'

'Which are limited,' she beamed at us. 'What I'd give to be a fly on that wall!'

'He'll be off to the Palace soon.'

'To concede defeat—' Her eyes filled with tears and she dropped into a chair.

'Miriam—'

'I'm alright,' she smiled. 'Happy crying. I'm alright.'

'You're tired out.'

No-one had worked harder than Miriam this past few weeks,

campaigning all day every day, marshalling teams of volunteers, organising meetings and rallies. She had her reward today, though. Beyond her wildest dreams.

'Shall I get you a cup of tea?' Tom asked.

'Tea?' she laughed. 'This is no time for tea. Where's the beer?'

'Oh, I can do better than that, my dear,' I laughed. 'Where are the bottles, Tom?'

We hadn't come empty-handed. My father had cleared his cellar early in the war, to save it from the bombs, but not before I'd set aside a crate or two for moments like this. What better time to pop a few corks?

We drank champagne, toasting the new world order. Harry should be here to share this, I thought. He deserved to be here, more than most. Tom caught my eye and I knew he was thinking the same. 'Absent friends,' he said, and we had a little toast of our own.

'Did you hear about the Labour candidate for Westminster?' asked Miriam. 'Jeremy Hutchinson. Safe Tory seat, of course, even on a day like today. But he canvassed No 10. Marched up Downing Street, knocked on the door and asked for a Mr Churchill.' She laughed. 'That's the spirit!'

The pundits had been so sure that the country would rally round Churchill and the papers ran cover to cover cheerleading for the Tories, day after day, but none of it worked. After all the lies in the press and everything power had to throw at Labour, here we were, toasting the victory of hope. I reached for Tom's hand.

'Let's go to Ealing,' I said. 'Let's go and see Rose and Nora.'

There was nowhere else to be on this day of days.

*

It was the summer break, so I expected the school to be empty, but I was wrong. The girls were away, but it seemed that every Socialist in London was there. Daisy was standing in the doorway, with a bottle of beer in her hand. She lived at the school now, in my old room, since her house took a direct hit from a doodlebug.

'Couldn't save a thing,' she told me. 'Everything gone but the memories.'

Humph had died before then, his lungs finally giving way in the terrible winter of 1940, when the Thames froze for the first time in decades and snow blew through the shattered windows of bombed-out houses, to lay undisturbed on abandoned furniture like dust sheets.

Daisy sang at his funeral in Honor Oak Cemetery. Millie Winsome, the film star, stood at the graveside with her sister Lilly, now Lady Crabbe, and crowds of Music Hall friends from all over the country. Sylvia Pankhurst was there, and an honour guard of old army comrades carried the coffin. A big gathering for a quiet man.

'He was loved,' said Daisy.

She went back to the little terraced house in Camberwell, with the walls full of theatrical posters and Humph's slippers propped against the fender and lived there alone till the street was wiped out during the Blitz. She was away when it happened, working with ENSA, touring a play to bases in Europe. 'Every Night Something Awful,' she laughed, when she told us about the show. Not so awful as the night the bombs fell on Camberwell. She came home to a pile of rubble and had lived at the school ever since.

She was in her sixties now, still looking twenty years younger, her red hair blazing in the sunlight, in the middle of a story and surrounded by an appreciative audience. As we approached, she raised her beer and beamed at us.

'Welcome. Is that champagne?' Tom held up the bottles he was carrying. 'Even more welcome!' she said and stood back to let us in.

Behind her, the house was packed and noisy. There was a wireless on full blast in the Common Room and somewhere in the distance, a chorus of 'The Red Flag' was raising the roof. There were people everywhere, sitting on the stairs, leaning in doorways, shouting over the din, laughing and hugging. A few couples were trying to dance in the hallway though there was no music and no space to move. They swayed together in the rainbow light of the stained- glass windows and I thought of Harry's kisses, long ago, in another life. The kitchen door swung open, as it had then, but it was Rose, not Nora, holding a plate of sandwiches.

'It's Spam and there's no butter but there's chutney from our apples. Help yourselves.' The revellers cleared the plate as fast as drinkers do. Rose saw Tom and I, pushed her way to us and threw her arms wide. 'I'm so glad you're here. What a day!'

'I'll get these bottles opened.' Tom headed off and Rose and I smiled at each other over our clasped hands.

'Where did he get champagne?'

'A gift from my father. In a manner of speaking.'

'It's stolen?'

'Redistributed,' I laughed. 'If not today, when?'

She hugged me. 'Isn't it wonderful? I still can't believe it. Come and see Nora.'

She led me through to the kitchen which was crammed full of people and lots of familiar faces. Annie Parker, all grown up now, was slicing bread at the table. She gave me the same old cheeky smile when she saw me.

'Hello, Miss.'

'It's Charlie to you now, Annie. How many times?'

'Can't get used to it, Miss.'

Annie had been at Bletchley Park for the duration, part of a head-hunted group of geniuses, doing something she couldn't tell us about. Awfully hush-hush. Little Annie Parker, helping to win the war and save the world.

Nora was in the pantry, reaching down jars from a supply on the top shelf.

'We're down to bread and jam now,' she called over her shoulder.

'Ain't rationing great?' grinned Annie.

Tom was handing out the fizz.

'Come and have some bubbly.'

Nora deposited half a dozen jam jars on the table and took a glass. Rose and I did the same. The four of us drew together in the busy kitchen and raised our hands.

'To Harry,' said Tom.

I looked across at Nora, waiting for the spasm of pain in her eyes, but today, it didn't come. Instead, she took a drink and we all followed suit.

'How he would have loved this,' I said, and she smiled, the smile that softens her face and draws you in. My heart felt suddenly lighter than it had for years. It's allowed, I thought. I'm allowed to be happy.

176

A cheer went up in the Common Room and Daisy popped her head around the door.

'Clem's on his way to the Palace. His wife's driving him in the family car. What a diamond!'

Clement Attlee, the quiet man who cared little for money and position, who was driven by ideals, not personal ambition. He took on the Tory press, said that Beaverbrook was the only truly evil man he ever met, and asked the voters if they wanted the country to be run by Parliament or by Fleet Street. His message was that the nation could come together to work for the benefit of all its people, not just the powerful few. And the people listened to him, remembered the desperation of the twenties and thirties and voted for change.

Rose raised her glass again.

'A Labour government.'

'I'll drink to that,' said Daisy. 'Hand one over.'

Glasses, bottles and mugs were raised all over the kitchen and the toast rang out.

'A Labour government!'

Someone started singing 'The Red Flag' again and everyone joined in, in every room of the house.

The people's flag is deepest red,
It shrouded oft our martyred dead.
And 'ere their limbs grew stiff and cold,
Their hearts' blood dyed its every fold.

Nora signalled to Rose, Daisy and I to follow her out into the garden and we did as she asked, gathering under a laburnum tree, heavy with yellow blossom, on the back lawn.

So, raise the scarlet banner high.
Beneath its shade, we'll live or die.

We stood in a little circle. The evening sun was golden bright, catching the fine lines on her face and the greys in her hair, but the pain she had carried for too long seemed softened, at last. She looked at each of us in turn before she spoke.

'I want to say sorry. You all kept fighting for this day and I let you down.'

Rose moved in and put an arm round her.

'No need for sorry,' said Daisy.

'We understood,' I added. 'We all understood.'

'No. I was wrong. Here we are today and, yes, we all know the struggle isn't over—the powerful lost the election but they won't let go without a fight. It will be two steps forward, one step back—and some of our own will sabotage like they always do—we know all of that but—'

'But the day came,' said Rose.

'Yes, it did.'

'We won.'

'Yes, we bleedin' did, comrades.' Daisy punched the air and we all laughed as the last lines of the song floated out of the house.

Though cowards flinch and traitors sneer
We'll keep the red flag flying here.

*

The crowds had thinned out, staggered home or moved on to other festivities and we sat around the kitchen table, drinking tea, as we had done so many times before. Tom was gone, on his way down to Central Hall for the official celebration.

'Clem's going to make his first speech as Prime Minister!' he pulled at me, happy and tipsy. 'Come on.'

But I wanted to stay where I was, to celebrate in this place, with these people.

'You go. You can tell me all about it later.'

So, he had joined a jubilant group in the street, waving wildly over the hedge as they left.

'Are you two having a thing?' Daisy asked me as we walked back into the house.

'We were,' I said. 'It's over now.'

'Shame.'

'Not really.'

She looked me in the eye and smiled.

'Fun whilst it lasted, eh?'

'Yes.'

'Fair enough. I had my share of that.'

'But then you settled down.'

'That was my choice. Doesn't have to be yours. As long as you're happy.'

I returned her smile.

'I am. I will be. I believe I will be.'

Rose and Nora were sitting, fingers entwined, and Daisy clasped their hands in both of hers.

'I had a telegram earlier, from Sylvia.'

'Is she still in Ethiopia?'

'No, she's back home in Woodford. She gets to celebrate a Labour government in Churchill's constituency. How sweet is that?'

'I heard Haile Selassie gave her a medal.'

'Two! The Foreign Office were spitting feathers. They hate her campaigning in Africa.'

' "That confounded Pankhurst woman," they call her.'

'She doesn't change.'

'Not a bit. The telegram said, "The long wait is over".'

We all smiled at that and Daisy raised her teacup.

'Sylvia Pankhurst,' she said, and we joined her toast.

'What's the best thing about the win?' I asked. 'What gives you most cause for hope?'

It was Rose who spoke first.

'One of our old girls is an MP now. Three are journalists on national newspapers, two work for the BBC, one is Dean of an Oxford college. Many are teachers and lawyers, artists and scientists. And there'll be more.' She smiled. 'If that isn't cause for hope, what is?'

'I couldn't read till I was twenty-eight,' said Daisy. 'Now Ellen Wilkinson is Minister for Education and we're bringing in free secondary schooling for every kid in the country. Information is power, comrades. What's not to like?'

It was Rose's turn to raise a cup.

'Ellen Wilkinson.'

We all drank to Ellen and I looked round the table, from Daisy to Rose to Nora. There are people we know we'll never lose, wherever we go, whatever happens. They run through our lives like mile markers, like signposts. They shape us. They are the voices in our heads, the faces we see when we close our eyes. That's the best legacy we can hope for. To pass it on.

'You now, Nora,' said Daisy. 'What's the best thing?'

'That's easy. The Health Service. When I was a kid, our neighbour Bridget died of cancer.' Her face clouded with the memory. 'She screamed in agony for weeks. No doctor, no treatment, no painkillers. It wasn't the first time I'd heard screaming like that. It was the sound of living and dying poor. But it was the first time I was old enough to know what was happening and I'll never forget it. The Health Service will change the world for working people. If it's the only thing we do with this majority, it'll be enough.'

'The Tories will fight it,' said Rose. 'Lots of doctors will too.'

'If anyone can do it, Nye Bevan can.'

'It'll happen.' Daisy threw out her arms. 'That's the joy of a fuck-you majority! Sorry, Rose.'

'Why just me?' Rose laughed.

'Well, you're a lady. Not common like me and Nora. And Charlie's young and modern. She don't mind.' She looked at me. 'Do you?'

'Not a bit.'

'There you go.'

'What's your hope then, Charlie?' Nora asked.

I thought of Old Nichol Street and the day when the scales fell from my eyes. The slums I was so ashamed of had been fire-bombed in the Blitz and reduced to smouldering ruins and now the survivors of our miserable buildings needed housing. All across the country, all the filthy, disease-ridden hovels lining the pockets of the landlords would be swept away by Labour's new broom.

'We're going to build houses,' I said. 'The Tories wouldn't even provide the basic human dignity of decent shelter. But we will.'

'Too right.' Daisy shook her head. 'Stone me, I still can't really believe it! All these years beating against a locked door. All the lies and the propaganda and people falling for it, time after time.'

'But not this time.'

'No. At long, bleedin' last!'

Rose yawned and stretched.

'It's late but I don't want to go to bed. I don't want this day to be over.'

180

'There'll be plenty more days,' said Nora.
'And lots to do.'
'Aye.'
'Time for one more song,' I said. 'Come on, Daisy.'
'What do you want?'
'You choose.'
'No contest then.'
She started to sing.

History is full of examples
Of the rich exploiting the poor
Of the powerful having their way at any cost
But it's also full of people
Who refused to be bowed down
Because the fight isn't over till it's lost.

It was the closing song from *One Foot in Front of the Other*.
Harry's anthem, the creed he lived by. And died by. Through
the blur of tears, I saw Rose and Nora's eyes were wet too. But
it was alright. We were alright.

Every stand you take
Is a drop of water in the stream
And one day the stream will be a flood.
Those who came before us
Taught that lesson well.
It's written in their tears and in their blood.

We can't choose the life we're given
But we can choose the life we live,
We can choose not to break, but to bend.
What we learn from those before us
What we give to those who follow
That's what matters in the end.

'Sing with me,' said Daisy and we all joined in the last verse.

When wrong is done
You have a choice,
You can be silent

Or you can raise your voice,
You can take action
Or you can take flight,
You can choose what's easy
Or do what's right.

Drops of water in the stream. Ripples that wear away the stone. That's what's required of us. That's our task. It sounds easy and sometimes it feels impossible. But what else is there?

2003

IT is nothing like the sacred battlefields of Flanders or the Normandy beaches. For years, under Franco, the Republican dead were actively forgotten. Graves were desecrated, humble monuments destroyed. There is no homage to the past at Jarama, until you look closely at the ground beneath your feet and see a spent bullet casing, then another, then hundreds of them scattered among the rubble, half-buried in the earth they fell on, untouched for decades.

The valley is etched through low hills covered in olive groves and wild sage, an expanse of rusty earth and rocks, peppered with tufts of dry gorse. Tall, slim trees grow right to the edge of the river, their roots in the silt, their sparse leaves glowing lime green in the sunlight. The only sound is the ripple of water on stone.

Charlie is sitting on a lichen-spotted boulder at the river's edge, a small figure in an empty landscape. Torn between a reluctance to intrude and an impulse to hug her close, Margaret hovers at a distance, waiting for an invitation.

'They sang "The Internationale" as they marched here.' Charlie gazes out across the valley. 'Tom said, when they blasted it out together it sounded like Bedlam! But their faces blazed with what it meant to them.'

She holds out a hand and Margaret takes it, holds it in both her own, her chest tight with love and sympathy, needing to comfort and not knowing how.

'Is this too hard?' she asks.

'He's here somewhere. His bones are here. He bled to death, frightened and in pain, without me to hold him.'

She sits next to Charlie. There are feathery grasses growing out of the water. When the breeze touches them, they shed their seeds in a flurry of gold that rises weightless and drifts away.

'Tell me what you want.' Charlie turns to her suddenly, with a new energy. 'How do we make it better?'

'What?'

'Everything. What should they have done with that '97 land-slide that was pissed up the wall?'

Margaret shakes her head.

'Not now Charlie. Not here.'

'Where better than here?'

Among the hopeful dead.

'It isn't anything you don't already know.'

'I want to hear it from you. Here. In this place. I want it said out loud.'

The arguments that New Labour dismisses with cynical certainty, the arguments that have always divided the left, the same old arguments. But for Charlie, and for Harry, I say it again.

'I want real change. A system that works for everybody, not just the entitled, greedy few. And I want the Labour Party to want it, to believe it's possible and not be afraid to say so. I want to hear the accepted myths challenged. I want some outrage!'

Charlie is smiling.

'Tony Benn tried that,' she says. 'And Michael Foot. Look what happened to them.'

'An establishment shit-storm, I know. Spin and distortions. Even outright lies. Anything to dismantle their credibility.'

'Misinformation. George Orwell knew what he was talking about.'

'It's why Blair gets a free pass. Because they know he's no threat to their interests. But it isn't enough to do only what they allow us to do. It isn't nearly enough. Tinkering at the edges, dropping a few crumbs from the top table. New Labour might be happy with that—'

'Intensely relaxed, I believe.'

'God save us from Peter Mandelson!'

Charlie laughs out loud and it echoes across the water, star-tling a wading bird that takes flight and soars away down the valley. She cups Margaret's face in her hands.

'There it is.'

'What?'

'The light in your eyes. This is what you are, Margaret—a po-litical animal—an idealist—a fighter. You can't deny it.'

184

The evening sunlight glints gold on the rocks, the red earth beneath the hills glowing like embers. Margaret reaches into her pocket.

'I found a poem on an International Brigade website. There's a verse that I thought—that might help. I wrote it down.'

She offers the slip of paper and Charlie takes it. She reads out loud.

Not blindly fighting in another's war,
Lured by cheap promises and drugged with drums.
But clear-eyed, bravely, counting all the cost.
Knowing what might be won, what might be lost.

The words seem to hover in the air, over the land and above the water.

'That was him, wasn't it?' Margaret says. 'He counted all the cost.'

Charlie holds the paper to her chest, above her heart, folding her weathered old hands over it, as if in invocation.

'He was strong. And I was weak.' She closes her eyes briefly, takes a deep breath. 'I couldn't imagine my life without him. The thought of losing him filled me with absolute terror. It wasn't that I stopped believing in the struggle. It just couldn't compete with my need for him.'

'You were eighteen.'

Eyes open again, blue and misted with tears, she nods in assent.

'Young love. First love. It was too big for me. I lost myself.'

'So how did you find your way back?'

'I made a conscious choice.'

'I don't understand.'

Charlie takes a small box from the bag at her side.

'His mother, Nora, lost faith when she lost him,' she says. 'She had fought the fight all her life, Harry's politics came from her, she was my hero, my role model. But when he was killed, she stopped believing for a long time. I knew Harry would have wanted anything but that, would have been heartbroken to hear it. I couldn't let him be the reason I turned my back on hope. So, I chose not to.' Her face suddenly lights up with amusement. 'And I'm with Oscar Wilde—if you're going to hope, then do it on a grand scale!'

'You choose to hope?'

'Yes.'

'So, can we make a conscious choice to forgive ourselves?' Margaret asks.

'I think we have to, my dear. No-one else can do it.' She opens the box. There are dried petals inside it, once red but faded now to sepia. They crumble like old paper as she empties them onto her palm. 'These were the first flowers he ever bought me. Red tulips for my birthday.'

'You kept them all this time?'

Charlie pushes herself upright and takes Margaret's arm.

'And now I'm letting them go.'

They walk the few steps to the river's edge and stand together as Charlie opens her fingers, as the dusty petals fall into the water and the swirl and eddy of the current catches them and carries them away.

Back at the hotel, they eat dinner in a verdant courtyard open to the night sky.

'Thank you for being here, my dear.'

'Thank you for asking me.'

'I wish you'd known him.'

'I feel I do, a little.'

Charlie smiles across the table.

'I loved him with all my heart. I was happy with the others, I loved some of them, but Harry was the one.'

'I'm so sorry you lost him.'

'But I had him before I lost him. How many people never have that? How many others have lost their hearts in war? I'm not alone. And I've had a good life. Different from how it might have been, but a full one.'

The rhythm of flamenco guitar in a nearby bar mingles with the drone of the cicadas high in the trees. Margaret watches Charlie scrape the last crusted grains of saffron rice from the paella pan and eat them slowly. She is pleasantly drowsy, lulled by good food and the warm breeze.

'Is David the one?'

In an instant, everything changes. This pilgrimage for Charlie has succeeded in keeping her own life at arm's length for a few days but, all in a moment, it is back and insistent, pressing on her chest, squeezing her heart.

'Yes. He is.'

'Lucky you.'

'Yes.'

Stupid. Stupid, selfish woman. To make a life then wilfully destroy it.

'How does he feel about the baby?'

She takes a deep breath.

'It's complicated.'

'He knows you're pregnant?'

'Yes.'

'And?'

Stupid. Stupid.

'It isn't his.'

'Oh, Margaret.'

'I've made such a mess of everything.'

The waitress arrives to clear their plates and they fall silent. Margaret feels Charlie's eyes on her but doesn't look up. David's face is in her mind, his voice in her head.

What matters is I love you.

When they are alone again, she forces the words out.

'I fell apart after I left my job. I was impossible to live with. It wasn't David—it was all me. But he agreed to a separation because he didn't know what else to do.'

'And then?'

'It only lasted a few weeks and I ran home. But by then I'd had a desperate one-night stand with an old boyfriend—'

'Oh, my dear.'

'When I realised I was pregnant, I couldn't function. I thought about having a secret abortion, not telling anyone and pretending it never happened, but I couldn't do it. I couldn't live that lie.'

'So you told him?'

The music stops with a last, wild chord and the sudden quiet is unsettling. The tables around them are empty but she feels exposed and unprotected. Her voice is barely audible.

'At first he couldn't look at me.'

The pain of others. The pain we cause. There is nothing worse.

'Then he said we could make it work. We could let it destroy us or decide not to be destroyed.'

Charlie beams.

'Exactly.'

Margaret sits up in her chair, making the connection.

'That's what you were talking about, isn't it? That's what you meant?'

'Absolutely.'

'But can I be selfish enough to let him do it? Do I want a child that isn't David's? Do I want to be a mother at all? I've been driving myself insane with it! One day I just packed a bag and ran. I went to the airport and the next plane was to Athens—'

'And here we are.'

'What should I do, Charlie? I need some wise words.'

Charlie holds out a hand. She is wearing a ring that Margaret has seen before, a blue-green stone in an old setting.

'Nora was given this ring by her friend, Daisy, after they were on hunger strike together in Holloway. And when the terrible news came from Spain, she gave it to me. It's aquamarine. For courage.' She slips it off her finger and holds it out. 'It's yours now.'

Margaret's eyes fill with tears.

'I don't know what to do. Tell me what to do.'

'Do what you have to do and live with the consequences. Whatever you decide about the baby, you make peace with the past and fight for the future.'

Margaret puts on the ring. When she moves her hand, the stone catches the light from the candle on the table and glows with colour from within.

'Did Nora ever get her faith back?' she asks.

'Eventually. When Labour got its landslide in the '45 election, Nora opened her heart to hope again. Not so shiny and unblemished as before, perhaps. But tried and tested and resolute.'

'What was it Tony Benn said? We fight the same battles over and over again.'

'He's right. We thought the new world order had arrived with Attlee's Labour, and, for a while, it seemed it had. We built the Welfare State, transformed the lives of working people, made real progress.'

'And look at us now.'

'It isn't all gone, but it will be if we aren't vigilant.'

'It's exhausting.'

With a twinkle in her eyes, Charlie reaches out and pats Margaret's hand.

'As I recall, Tony Benn also said toughen up. Bloody toughen up.'

'Point taken,' Margaret smiles.

'Continuity. We are links in a chain. No more, no less.'

'There's comfort in that.'

'And responsibility. Pass it on. That's another thing Nora taught me.'

'No pressure then.'

Charlie laughs, her lined old face young with mischief.

'Don't worry, my dear. We can have dessert first.'

*

They are on a high hillside. For the first time, Harry looks insubstantial, like a ghost, like a dream.

'Are you sorry you loved me?' he asks.

'Never for a second,' she tells him.

'I'm sorry for leaving you.'

'I know.'

The wind is tugging at her clothes, blowing her hair across her face. It doesn't touch him. Everything about him is still.

'Can you forgive me now?'

'Where are your glasses?'

'I take them off when things get rough, remember?'

He is smiling. She loves him completely.

'Can you forgive me?' she asks.

'There's no blame. It is what it is.'

'But was it worth it?'

His smile fades, only a shadow of it lingers in his eyes.

'Harry?'

'Don't ask me that,' he says.

*

At Delphi, I watched an archaeological dig in progress. They worked with brushes on an inch or two of ground, gently scraping away the years to reveal the hidden remains of ancient lives. Looking at the artefacts, I saw myself, buried in the dark but being brought by inches into

189

the light. It's as if Charlie has been working on me with a fine brush and here I am, emerging from the accumulation of years.

My mother's first job was washing dishes in a hotel kitchen, standing on a crate because she was too small to reach the sink. She passed the eleven-plus for grammar school but there was no money for a uniform and her wage was needed at home. So her education ended.

My mother was as fierce for my future as only one deprived of her own could be. Sometimes, when I think of her, I see behind her all the generations of my family, who lived without choice because of an accident of birth.

My grandfather was buried alive in a pit explosion when he was fifteen. His father and brothers dug him out with their bare hands, pulling him through a narrow opening which scraped the skin from his back as he squeezed through. The scars healed blue with coal dust. He was tattooed a miner.

Nothing unusual. Similar stories lie behind millions of lives.

So much stolen from so many.

How can we rest before justice is done?

Back on the terrace, Charlie is in her cardigans, the sea is lapping the shingle and Margaret feels like she has come home after a long absence.

'How are you?' she asks.

'Wiser.' Charlie smiles.

'Impossible.'

'Ah. Apparently not.'

'It helped then, going to Spain?'

'Yes. I should have gone years ago.'

'I think maybe you weren't ready till now.'

Charlie laughs.

'Now who's wise?'

'Well, you taught me everything I know.'

The news starts on the radio. Charlie moves to switch it off, but Margaret stops her.

'No,' she says. 'Let's hear it.'

Silence changes nothing.

The headline is the latest report from the Iraq Survey Group. No evidence of WMDs, it says, despite a search, costing three hundred million dollars and rising.

'An expensive lie,' says Charlie.

190

'There's always money for war.'

'How long since Bush announced "Mission Accomplished"? Four months and no sign of it ending.'

'It could go on for years. We've started something we don't know how to finish.'

'This is what they'll be remembered for.' Charlie's eyes flame with anger. 'Small comfort for Iraq but this will be Bush and Blair's legacy. This is where history will judge them.'

'History isn't soon enough for me.'

Charlie turns her head.

'Meaning?'

'A wise woman once asked me if you stop fighting for right because wrong is winning.'

'And do you?'

Margaret smiles a slow smile. 'Apparently not.'

'Oh, my dear.' Charlie's face lights up with delight. 'You're ready.'

'I wouldn't go that far. But I'm willing.'

Charlie gets to her feet, a small figure against the glare of sun on water, her white hair blowing in the breeze, her eyes as blue as the sky.

'All will be well, my dear. Give me a hug.'

And Margaret opens her arms to Charlie, the soft skin and hard old bones, all the comfort and inspiration that she is, gathered in gratefully and greedily.

'You saved me.'

'Nonsense.'

'Yes, you did. Thank you.'

'And thank you, Margaret.'

'I didn't do anything.'

'You found your courage. And inspired me to do the same.'

'I'm still scared to death.'

'It isn't courage if you aren't afraid. Small acts, remember.'

'Yes.'

'We've had good times, haven't we?'

'The best.'

'Was Greece what you expected?'

'Much more. I didn't expect you.' Margaret looks down at the ring on her finger. The aquamarine echoes the blues and greens of the mosaic tiles at her feet, broken fragments re-made into a different whole. 'I spoke to David this morning.'

'And?'

'I'm keeping the baby.'

'Oh, my dear.'

They smile at each other across the table. Margaret puts a hand on her belly and leaves it there for a long, still moment.

'Charlie. He or she will be called Charlie.'

There's someone on the beach who whistles just like you, a breathy tune, an old familiar song. I look up, shading my eyes from the sun, knowing the silhouette by the sparkling water isn't you but wanting it to be. Imagining it is.

I miss you, David. You are alone in our home, sleeping alone in our bed, waiting for my step in the hall.

I feel a sudden longing for cold air and log fires. For my own hearth. One foot in front of the other.

The unknowable, demanding future.

I choose hope.

ACKNOWLEDGEMENTS

M Y heartfelt gratitude to Kate and Ian for giving so freely of their time and expertise to make the dream a reality, to Vicky for her meticulous work and to Julie for the constant flame of hope that warms everyone it touches.

My late mum and dad, Belle and Bill, have been much on my mind and in my heart whilst writing this.

Love and thanks to my closest and dearest, who have held me through the past year. Dec and Sue, Sarah, Hannah, Christine, and James, Eileen, Melanie, Amy, Jemma, Chris and Dan. And to Sally and Martyn, Carol, Peter, Annie and all the generous souls in the mighty village of Moniaive.

Most of all, to Mark, for a lifetime of support, encouragement and love.